RANDOM HOUSE
HOUSE

LARGE
PRINT

**Also by Kristin Hannah
available from
Random House Large Print**

Between Sisters
The Things We Do for Love

Comfort & Joy

KRISTIN HANNAH
Comfort & Joy

A NOVEL

RANDOM HOUSE
LARGE PRINT

Copyright © 2005 by Kristin Hannah
Excerpt from **Magic Hour** copyright © 2006
by Kristin Hannah
All rights reserved.
First Edition, 2005

Published in the United States of America by
Random House Large Print in association with
Ballantine Books, New York.
Distributed by Random House, Inc., New York.

This book contains an excerpt from the forthcoming hardcover edition of **Magic Hour** by Kristin Hannah. This excerpt has been set for this edition only and may not reflect the final content of the forthcoming edition.

The Library of Congress has established a Cataloging-in-Publication record for this title.

ISBN-13: 978-0-375-43539-3
ISBN-10: 0-375-43539-5

www.randomlargeprint.com

FIRST LARGE PRINT EDITION
10 9 8 7 6 5 4 3 2 1

This Large Print edition published in accord with the standards of the N.A.V.H.

For Benjamin

Comfort & Joy

Part One

"It's a dangerous business . . . going out of your door. You step into the Road, and if you don't keep your feet, there's no knowing where you might be swept off to."

—J. R. R. TOLKIEN

ONE

Christmas parties are the star on the top of my "don't" list this year. Other things to avoid this season: Ornaments. Trees. Mistletoe (definitely). Holiday movies about families. And memories.

Memories most of all. Last year, I celebrated Christmas morning in my own living room, with the two people I loved most in the world. My husband, Thomas, and my sister, Stacey.

A lot can change in twelve months.

Now, I am in my kitchen, carefully packing frosted Santa cookies into Tupperware containers, layering wax paper between each row. On a strip of masking tape, I write my name in bold black letters: Joy Candellaro. When I'm done, I dress for work in a pair of black jeans and a bright green sweater set. At the last moment, I add little wreath earrings. Perhaps if I **look** festive, people will stop asking me how I am doing. Balancing the pale pink containers in my arms, I lock up my house and make my way to the garage. As I round the hood of the car, I sidle past the row of file cabinets that line the back wall. My dreams are in those metal drawers, organized with the kind of care only a librarian can manage.

I have saved every scrap I've ever read about exotic locales and faraway places. When I read the words and see the pictures, I dream of having an adventure.

Of course, I've been dreaming of that for ten years now, and since I've been single again for almost three months, and separated from Thom for eight months before that, it's safe to say I'm a dreamer not a doer. In fact, I haven't added to my files or opened one of the cabinets since my divorce.

I ease past them now and get into my sensible maroon Volvo. Behind me, the garage door opens, and I back down the driveway.

It is still early in the morning on this last Friday before Christmas. The street lamps are on; light falls from them in cones of shimmering yellow through the predawn shadows. As my car rolls to a stop at the bottom of the driveway, the headlights illuminate my house. It looks . . . faded in this unnatural light, untended. The roses I love so much are leggy and bare. The planters are full of dead geraniums.

A memory flashes through me like summer thunder: there and gone.

I come home from work early . . . see my husband's car is in the driveway. The roses are in full, riotous bloom.

I remember thinking I should cut some for an arrangement.

In the house, I toss my coat on the

maple bench and go upstairs, calling out his name.

I am halfway up the stairs when I recognize the sounds.

In my mind and my memories, I kicked the door open. That's what I told people later. The truth was, I barely had the strength to push it open.

There they are, naked and sweating and rolling, in my bed.

Like an idiot, I stand there, staring at them. I thought he'd **feel** my presence as keenly as I'd always felt his, that he'd look up, see me and—oh, I don't know, have a heart attack or burst into tears and beg for my forgiveness or beg for forgiveness **while** having a heart attack.

Then I see her face, and a bad moment rounds the bend into horrific. It is my sister.

Now there's a "For Sale" sign in front of my house. It's been there for months, but who am I kidding? A wrecked marriage scares everyone. It's like a rock tossed into a still blue pond; the ripples go on and on. No one wants to buy this house of bad luck.

I hit the gas too hard and back out into the street, putting the memories in my rearview mirror.

If only they would stay there. Instead, they're like passengers, crowding in on me, taking up too much air.

No one knows what to say to me anymore, and I can hardly blame them. I don't know what I want to hear, either. In the school library, where I work, I hear the whispers that grind to a halt at my entrance and notice how uncomfortable the ensuing silences can be.

I make it easy on my friends—or try to—by pretending that everything is okay. I've been doing that a lot this year. Smiling and pretending. What else can I do? People have grown tired of waiting for me to get over my divorce. I know I need to glide onto the track of my old life, but I can't seem to manage it; neither do I have the courage to form a new one, though, in truth, it's what I want. It's what I've wanted for a long time.

At the corner, I turn left. The streets of Bakersfield are quiet on this early morning. By the time I reach the high school, it is just past seven o'clock. I pull into my parking space, gather my cookies, and go inside.

At the main desk, the school secretary, Bertha Collins, smiles up at me. "Hey, Joy."

"Hey, Bertie. I brought some cookies for tonight's faculty party."

Her look turns worried. "Aren't you coming?"

"Not this year, Bertie. I don't feel too festive."

She eyes me knowingly. As a twice-divorced woman, she thinks she understands, but she can't, not really. Bertie has three kids and two parents and four sisters. My own math doesn't add up that way. "Take care of yourself, Joy. The first Christmas after a divorce can be . . ."

"Yeah. I know." Forcing a smile, I start moving. In the past year, this technique has worked well for me. Keep moving. I walk down the hallway, turn left at the empty cafeteria and head for my space. The library.

My assistant, Rayla Goudge, is already at work. She is a robust, gray-haired woman who dresses like a gypsy and tries to write all her notes in haiku. Like me, she is a graduate of U.C. Davis with a teaching certificate. We have worked side by side for almost five years and both enjoyed every minute. I know that in May, when she finishes her master's degree in library science, I will lose her to another school. It's one more change I try not to think about.

"Morning, Joy," she says, looking up from the pile of paperwork in front of her.

"Hey, Ray. How's Paul's cold?"

"Better, thanks."

I store my purse behind the counter and begin my day. First up are the computers. I go from one to the next, turning them on for the students, then I replace yesterday's newspapers with todays. For the next six hours, Rayla and I work side by side—checking the catalog system, generating overdue notices, processing new books, and re-shelving. When we're lucky, a student comes in for help, but in this Internet age, they are more and more able to do their school research at home. Today, of course, on this last school day before the winter break, the library is as quiet as a tomb.

That is another thing I try not to think about: the break. What will I do in the two and one-half weeks I have off?

In past years, I have looked forward to this vacation. It's part of the reason I became a school librarian. Fifteen years ago, when I was in college, I imagined traveling to exotic locales in my weeks off.

"Joy, are you okay?"

I am so lost in memories of Before that it takes me a second to realize that

Rayla is speaking to me. I'm standing in the middle of the library, holding a worn, damaged copy of **Madame Bovary**.

The bell rings: The walls seem to vibrate with the sound of doors opening, kids laughing, feet moving down the hall.

The winter break has begun.

"Do you need a ride to thc party?" Rayla asks, coming up to me.

"The party?" I say, as if I'm actually thinking about it. "No, thanks."

"You're not coming, are you?"

Rayla has always been able to do that: pierce my defenses with a look. "No."

"But . . ."

"Not this year, Ray."

Rayla sighs. "So, what will you do tonight?"

We both know that the first night of our vacation is special. Last year, on this Friday evening, Stacey and I met up for dinner and went to the mall, where I agonized over the perfect gift for Thom.

It turned out to be my sister.

Those are exactly the kind of memories I try to avoid, but they're like asbestos: invisible and deadly. You need special gear to get rid of them.

Rayla touches my arm. "Have you put up a tree yet?"

I shake my head.

"I could help you decorate one."

"No, thanks. I need to do it myself."

"And will you?"

I look down into her kind gray eyes and find it surprisingly easy to smile. "I will."

She loops an arm through mine. Together, we walk through the quiet library and emerge into the crowded, busy hallways of the high school. All around us kids are laughing and talking and high-fiving one another.

In the parking lot, Rayla walks me to my car. There, she stops and looks up at me. "I hate to leave you alone for the holidays. Maybe Paul and I should cancel our trip to Minnesota."

"Don't you dare. Enjoy your family. I'll be fine."

"You and Stacey . . ."

"Don't," I say sharply, and then whisper: "Please."

"She and Thom will break up, you'll see. She'll come to her senses."

I have lost count of the times Rayla has said this to me, and of the times I've said it to myself.

"Why don't you go to one of those dream places of yours—like Machu Picchu or London?"

"Maybe I will," I say. It's what I always say. We both know the truth: I'm scared to go alone.

Rayla pats my hand and kisses my cheek. "Well. I'll see you in January, Joy."

"Merry Christmas, Rayla."

"And to you."

I watch her walk to her car and drive away. Finally, I get into my own front seat and sit there, staring through the windshield. When I start the engine, the radio comes on. It's an instrumental rendition of "Upon a Midnight Clear" that immediately reminds me of better times in previous years. My mom loved this song.

Rayla is right. It's time for me to get started on Christmas. There's no more putting it off. Smiling and pretending will not get me through the holidays. It's time for me to embark on this new single life of mine.

The traffic out of the high school is bumper to bumper with kids yelling out the window to one another, but by the time I reach Almond Street, the road is empty.

On Fifth Street, I turn left and pull into the lot beside a Chevron station, where Scout Troop #104 has set up their yearly tree sale. On this late Friday afternoon, I can see right away that the stock is pretty depleted, and frankly, there's more brown on these branches than green. In this part of California, the trees go bad fast and I've waited too long to get a prime choice.

I wander through the fake forest on the corner of Fifth and Almond, nodding now and then to friends and strangers, trying to pretend I'm picking out the perfect tree. In truth, I'm trying not to look at them too closely. Finally, I can't stand it anymore. I choose the tree to my left, find a kid to help me, and reach for my wallet.

The nice young boy scout who takes my money hands me a receipt and a Kleenex.

I'm crying. **Perfect.**

By the time the tree is strapped onto my car, I'm a basket case. Sniffling and crying and shaking.

I am still in bad shape when I pull up to the ATM machine, though, thankfully, there are no witnesses to my meltdown. On a whim, I withdraw two hundred and fifty dollars. If I'm going to put up this tree, I'll need all new ornaments. I can hardly use the ones I collected during my marriage. And I intend to buy myself a killer gift to open on Christmas morning.

The thought of spending money on myself should make me happy; it's not something we high school librarians do a lot.

At least that's what I tell myself as I turn into my neighborhood.

Madrona Lane is a pretty name for a pretty street in a not-so-pretty suburb of Bakersfield. I've always appreciated the irony of living on a street named for a tree that doesn't grow here; especially in view of the fact that the developers cut down every green thing that dared to grow on the block. When my husband and I first saw the house it was run down and neglected, the only home on the cul-de-sac with grass that needed cutting and a fence in need of paint. The realtor had seen all these as possibilities for a young couple such as us. "The previous owners," she'd whispered to me as I stepped through a patch of dry-rotted floor in the bathroom, "went through a terrible divorce. A real **War of the Roses** thing."

We'd all laughed at that. Of course, it turned out not to be so funny.

I am almost to my house when I see Stacey standing in my driveway, all by herself.

I slam on the brakes.

We stare at each other through the windshield. The minute she sees me, she starts to cry. It is all I can do not to follow suit.

She's come to tell you it's over with Thom. It's the moment I've been waiting for, but now that it's here, I don't know what to do. Without forgiveness, there's no future between Stacey and me, but how can I forgive a sister who slept with my husband?

I ease my foot back onto the accelerator and pull into the driveway. Then I get out of the car.

Stacey stands there, looking at me, clutching her ski coat around her. Tears glisten on her cheeks.

It's the first time we've really looked at each other since this nightmare began, and instead of anger, I feel an unexpected longing. I remember a dozen things about her, about **us,** just then, like our famous family road trip through the desert states. Hell in a Volkswagen bus with my mom singing Helen Reddy songs at the top of her lungs and smoking Eve cigarettes one after another.

I approach her slowly. As always, looking at my younger sister is like looking in a mirror. Irish twins; that's what our mom called us. We're less than twelve months apart in age and have the same curly copper-red hair, pale, freckled skin, and blue eyes. No wonder Thom fell for her; she's the younger, smiling version of me.

She takes one step toward me and starts to talk.

I'm leaving him.

It's a moment before I realize that that's not what she said. "What?" I say, stepping back, frowning.

"We can't go on like this," she says. "Not now. It's Christmas."

I feel upended somehow, confused. "I should forgive you because it's Christmas?"

"I know you won't forgive me, but it was over between you and Thom . . ."

"We were having problems . . ." I don't even know how to finish, what to say. None of this feels right.

Stacey bites her lower lip—a sign of nervousness from way back—then hands me a piece of thick white paper. I can tell instantly what it is.

A wedding invitation. The blessed event is set to take place on June sixth.

It hits me like a right hook to the jaw. "Y-you're kidding me, right? You should be breaking up with him . . . not marrying him."

Slowly, she opens her coat. She is dressed for the holidays in red velvet pants and a white knit top with Rudolph stitched in sequins on the front. "I'm pregnant," she says, touching a belly that's flatter than mine.

And there it is, finally, after months of pretending to be okay, the thing I can't handle. For five years, I have dreamed of having a baby; I used to beg Thom to start our family. He was never "ready." Now I know why. It was me. He didn't want to have a child with me.

She's crying harder now. "I'm sorry, Joy. I know how much you want a baby."

I want to scream at her, to shriek my pain, maybe even smack her, but I can't seem to breathe. Tears are blurring my vision; they're not ordinary tears, either. They actually hurt. I can't believe she'd do this to me. To us. How can two girls who used to be peas in a pod have come to this?

"I never wanted to hurt you . . ."

I can't listen anymore. One more blow and I'm afraid I'll go to my knees, right here in my driveway, and I've spent every day of the last year just trying to stand. I turn away from my sister and run to my car. A part of me can hear her yelling my name, calling out to me, but I don't care. The words are elongated somehow, stretched into meaningless sounds and syllables. Nothing makes sense.

I get into my car, start the engine and barrel backward, into the empty street.

I have no idea where I'm going and I don't care. All that matters is putting miles between me and that wedding invitation in my driveway and the baby growing in my sister's womb.

When I see the exit for the airport, it seems natural to turn off. Maybe even a destiny-at-work kind of thing. I park and go into the terminal.

It's small, but busy on this Friday. Lots of people obviously want to put miles between the heres and theres of their lives in the holiday season.

I look up at the departures board.

Hope.

A shiver goes through me; the word looks so out of place on the list, tucked as it is between ordinary cities like

Spokane and Portland. I blink and look again, just in case I've gone slightly mad and imagined it.

Hope remains. It's in British Columbia, apparently. Canada.

There's no line at the counter. I walk there slowly, still somehow waiting to wake up, but when I get there, a woman looks up at me.

"May I help you?"

"The flight to Hope . . . is there a seat?"

She frowns. "It's a charter. Just a second." She looks down at her computer screen. Fingernails click on the keys. "There are seats, but they were purchased in bulk." She glances around, catches sight of a heavy-set man dressed in camouflage fatigues. "Go talk to him."

Now, I'm not the kind of woman who strolls easily up to strange men, especially when they look like Burl Ives on a big game hunt, but this is no time for caution. I'm desperate. One more second in this town and I might start screaming.

For all I know, Stacey is still in my driveway, waiting for me to return so we can "talk" more. I clutch my purse under my arm and go to him.

"Excuse me," I say, trying—without much success—to smile. "I need Hope."

He grins at this. "There isn't a whole lot up there. For a city girl, I mean."

"Sometimes just getting away is enough."

"You don't have to tell me that twice. Well, we've got an extra seat, if you want it. Say one hundred dollars? But I can't promise you a way to get back. We're a play-it-by-ear bunch."

"Me, too." Normally, I'd laugh at that, it's so far from the truth, but just now it feels right. Besides, I'm not even sure I need a way to get back. Who knows? This is a tear in the fabric of my ordinary life. All I have to do is step through. And I have my Christmas money with me. "Do I need a passport?"

"Nope. Just your driver's license."

I can leave here, make a quick stop

and plane change in Seattle, show my identification, go through customs, and be in Hope by midnight. I make a decision to leave my own country in less time than it usually takes me to decide between packages of meat at my local Von's.

I whip out my wallet and find the cash. "I'm in."

TWO

An hour later, I am at the gate, holding a ticket to Hope. All around me, men are talking, laughing. There is an inordinate amount of high-fiving going on. They are trophy hunters I discover, the kind of guys who decorate with hooves. This is their big hunt, away from kids and wives, and it's clear that the party starts before the plane takes off. They're completely uninterested in the quiet, tired-looking woman in their midst. I sit down in one of the empty seats. Beside me is a magazine. **Hunting and Fishing News**. A librarian will read anything, so I pick it up and flip through the pages. An article on duck blinds leaves me cold, as does a series of how-to taxidermy photographs. Finally, I turn the page and find a pretty picture of an old-fashioned resort. It's called the Comfort Fishing Lodge and it welcomes me to come and stay awhile.

Stay awhile.

It's a lovely thought. I fold the flimsy magazine in half and shove it into my bag. When I get home, I'll file the article alongside my other dreams, alphabetically. Someday, I'd like to visit the Comfort Lodge. As I'm fitting the magazine in the cluttered bag, I feel the pebbled leather of my camera case. My fingers close around it, pulling it out of my purse.

No newfangled digital camera for me. This is the real thing. A heavy black and silver Canon SLR. I take it out of the case, slip the strap around my neck, and remove the lens cap.

If I'm finally taking a trip into the unknown; there ought to be photographs to document the momentous event.

I focus and snap on the gate, on the

other passengers, on the view of the run-
way through the dirty windows. I even
try to take a picture of myself. All of it oc-
cupies my mind for a while, but then the
real world creeps back into my thoughts.

Stacey is going to marry Thom and
have his child.

It hurts almost more than I can bear.
Tears sting my eyes again; I wipe them
away impatiently. I am so tired of crying,
so tired of feeling like half a person, but I
don't know how to change things. All I
know is that for more than three decades,
my sister has been the bedrock of my life,
and now I'm standing on sand. I have
never felt so lost and alone. If I could
simply blink my eyes and say a prayer to
disappear, I would.

They call my flight over the loud-
speaker; men surge forward like a flannel-
clad centipede, legs all moving at once. I
follow quietly behind them.

On the plane, I find an empty seat
in the last row. My armrest practically
touches the restroom door, it's so close. I

try not to see a metaphor in this placement. Instead, I sit down, strap myself in, and peer out the tiny oval window at the falling night. The men are all in the front of the plane, laughing and talking. In no time, we're cleared for flight and up we go, into the now black sky.

I flip through the hunting and fishing magazine again. An article on the Olympic rainforest grabs my attention. It's in Washington State, apparently tucked in between hundreds of miles of coastline and a jagged mountain range. The trees are gigantic, primeval, the greens absolute and somehow soothing. A woman could get lost in a place like that. I could take hundreds of glorious photographs, maybe even—

"You okay back here all by yourself?"

I look up.

It's Burl Ives again. He smiles at me: the movement bunches up his cattle-sweeper moustache and shows off a row of oversized dentures.

It's the last half of his question, the "all

by yourself," that gets me. "I'm okay," I say, though it's miles from true.

"I'm Riegert, by the way. Riegert Milosovich."

"It's nice to meet you. I'm Joy."

"Well. You have a great vacation, Joy. And wish us luck on the hunt."

"Stay safe," I say, unable to really hope the hunt goes well. I'm a card-carrying member of the don't-shoot living-things club. And the idea of men drinking and loading weapons seems remarkably stupid, but it's not my business. "And thanks again for the seat. I think a little Hope is exactly what I need."

"Don't we all?"

He ducks into the bathroom and slams the door shut. A few moments later, he's out again and heading up the aisle toward his seat. He is almost to the first row when I hear a noise and feel a shudder in the airplane. Riegert stumbles forward, falls to his knees.

The nose of the plane dips down.

Down.

That's not good. Planes should be headed up.

I grip the armrests to steady myself. I know it's ridiculous—I mean, I can't **hold** myself in place. But it makes me feel better, in control.

The plane levels off. I have time to murmur "thank God" and to smile before the explosion.

The plane drops hard and fast. My body flies forward; the seat belt yanks me back. I hit the cusions like a rag doll, with a terrible snap to the neck. My camera hits me in the ribs, hard. Bright yellow oxygen masks drop from the ceiling.

Somewhere in front of me, a man screams. It is a terrible sound, guttural and unnatural. I shake my head, thinking **NO!** Just that word. My heart is beating so fast I can't draw a breath.

In the front of the cabin, the flight attendant is telling us to bend forward and press our heads into the seat in front of us. She's pointing out the exit rows.

The captain interrupts her speech to

say, "Brace yourselves. Flight attendant: Take your seat."

This isn't turbulence.

We're going to **crash**. You'd think it would happen in the blink of an eye, a thing like this, an airplane falling out of the sky, but the truth is that every second feels like an hour. It's true that your life spirals before your eyes.

I call out my sister's name and double over, gasping in pain. I should have **talked** to her, let her talk to me. My fingers claw into the armrests. Every breath is ragged and sharp.

The captain says again, "Brace for landing."

Landing. They make it sound scheduled, as if . . .

The plane slams into the ground nose first.

This time my scream is lost in the screeching, shrieking whine of tearing metal.

Things fly past me—a row of seats, a suitcase, a tray. It's like being in a wind tunnel. The flight attendant tumbles past me. She is still strapped in her chair. All I can do is watch in horror as she goes past me, screaming. For a heartbeat, our gazes lock, then the cabin lights go out.

I scream again, unable this time to stop. The sounds I make are nothing, breezes in the monsoon.

Although I am seeing everything in slow motion, I know that the plane is rocketing forward, crashing through trees and rocks and dirt.

We hit something and flip over. My camera cracks me in the eye.

The whole plane shudders and groans and comes to a creaking stop.

A pain explodes in my head.

It takes me a second to realize we're upside down. I'm hanging from my seat belt and everything hurts. The pain in my head—right behind my left eye—is like a hot iron wedge being hammered in place. I can taste blood.

But we are stopped. The horrible

wrenching sound of metal tearing has stopped. Now it is quiet. Eerie.

Smoke rolls through the cabin, swallowing the seats and aisle. I can't see anything. The coughing starts, then the sobbing.

I unlatch my seat belt and fall to the floor, hitting my head so hard I lose consciousness for a moment. When I wake, I am disoriented. Then I taste my own blood and I remember: I need to get out of the plane.

But smoke is everywhere. I can see flames licking along the walls, zipping up fabric-covered seats. Hungry orange tongues . . . everywhere.

Coughing, I look around for something to hold over my nose and mouth.

There is nothing. The cabin is all darkness and smoke and flames. People are dropping from their seats, landing on what is now the floor. I take off my coat and hold it over my face as I crawl toward the exit—at least I hope it's an exit. All I know is I hear movement in front of me, coughing and footsteps and whispering. The ceiling is full of seams and bumps that scrape my knees. I bang my head on the overhead bins that have fallen open.

I feel my way through the thick smoke, pushing aside debris, past gaping holes where the side of the plane should be. At each new row, I look for people still in their seats, hanging unconscious, but I find no one.

Finally, after what seems to take hours, I see the opening. A man is there, holding out his hand, helping me out. He doesn't seem to know that his hair and shirt are matted with blood, that a spike of some kind is lodged in his upper arm. "This way," he says in a tired, shaking voice.

"You need a doctor," I say, surprised that I'm crying. The words release something in me, something so big I'm afraid I'll drown in it and be swept away. I finally stagger to a stand.

He touches my head. The fingers he

draws back are stained red. "So do you. Are you the last one?"

"I think so. I was in the last row." I turn to look back at my seat and see the gaping black and orange mouth that is what's left of the tail section.

How did I not notice that?

Shaking, my head aching now that I feel the blood leaking down my cheek, I take his hand. It's calloused and sweaty and makes me feel almost safe.

The darkness outside is absolute, velvet, nothing like the gray haze of the burning cabin.

The ground squishes beneath my feet, giving way beneath my steps. It's like quicksand, hard to walk in. I look down at my feet. Something feels wrong. As if gravity has been lost or changed somehow. I look for someone to ask, "Where are we?" This isn't the world we know. The air is harsh, different. The ground is soft. I wonder suddenly if it is blood that has softened the ground—our blood—or maybe it's gasoline.

Everyone is as dazed as I am. Over by the nearest tree, a group is beginning to form. How can I walk that far and why am I alone?

In the distance, I hear sirens.

I trip on something and fall to my knees. The pain in my head is back, throbbing.

I hear something and look up.

At first, I think it's the ambulances and police cars driving up, and then I think it's screaming . . . but that's past us. We survived.

It seems to take ages, but I climb to my feet once again. I'm upright; I try to hear. My head is pounding.

"Explode . . . Run."

Words. Someone is yelling. Smoke engulfs me, billowing from the tail.

"Run! It's going to explode." I see Riegert running toward me, waving his arms.

A second later his words register. I try to run through the spongy black ground, toward the forest.

But I'm too late, and I know it.

The blast, when it comes, is like nothing I've ever known.

One second I'm running for cover; the next I'm airborne, weightless. When I hit the ground it is in a thud of pain. Then everything is dark.

When I open my eyes, I find myself staring up at a Halloween sky, all black and gray with the hint of eerie flickering orange light. Tree tips fringe it all, form a strange circle overhead. They are not ordinary trees; they're giants. They ring the crash site like gargantuan visitors, whispering among themselves. A lackluster rain is falling; it's really more of a mist.

At first I can't hear anything except the beating of my own heart. It's as if my ears are stuffed with cotton. My heartbeat is a slow, thudding echo of distant sound.

Gradually, though, I hear more.

Sirens, muffled and seemingly far away, but recognizable. Engines purring. Tires crunching through gravel or rock.

Where am I?

The answer comes to me in a rush of images and a surge of adrenaline.

The plane.

Crashed.

My camera strap is strangling me. I wrench it free, gasping for breath.

The gray in the sky is smoke from the plane's explosion. All around me trees are on fire. That's the orange in the sky: flames. I can hear the crackling now, feel the heat. My cheeks are coated in blood and sweat.

I try to get up but I can't move.

I'm paralyzed.

I stare at my feet, trying not to panic. One foot is bare. No sock, no shoe; just dark, muddy toes pointed skyward.

"Wiggle," I manage to whisper.

My right foot does a spastic little dance.

I'm not paralyzed. **Thank you, God.**

It takes forever, but finally I move my arms, wedge them underneath me and sit up. From my hiding place in the trees, I can see the crash site.

The plane is an oblong bullet of fire, wingless. The grass around it is a lake of mud and ash and debris. Trees lay on their sides like giant, broken toothpicks. For the first time, I understand the concept of devastation. Ruin. This land is broken now, as bleeding as we are.

Far away, through the ashy smoke, I can see ambulances and police cars and fire trucks. The survivors are there, clustered in the bright glow of headlights and temporary lighting. I need to take a picture of this, document it, but my hands are shaking uncontrollably.

"I'm over here," I cry weakly, trying to raise my hand.

But no one is looking over here. No one is looking for me.

Why? I wonder. Then I remember Riegert calling out for me, reaching out, then covering his face at the blast and falling to the ground.

They think I died in the explosion.
But I'm here.
It is my last conscious thought.

I see her standing in the trees, not far away from me. She looks exactly as I remember: tall and thin, with silvery blond hair and eyes the exact color of a robin's egg. Her skin is pale and unlined still; she is wearing a pink Rocky Mountain Mama T-shirt and her favorite Max Factor lipstick. Strawberries and cream. I wait for her to smile, but she crosses her arms instead and glances away, as if she has another place to be. She is smoking a long, brown cigarette.

"Mom?" I say quietly, wondering if she can hear me. There is a strange cacophony of noise around us—motors running, high pitched wails that sound like sirens, a crackling that sounds like wax paper being balled up. Most of all I can hear my heart, though. It's running fast, skipping so many beats I feel light-headed.

She moves toward me, almost gliding. As she gets closer, I see her smile—finally—and it releases something in me.

She kneels beside me. "You're hurt."

I know she is touching my forehead. I can see her movement, but I can't feel her touch. I stare into the eyes I love so much. Until now, this moment, I had begun to forget how she looked, the gentleness of her touch, the sound of her voice.

Her hands on my face are so cool, so comforting. "Wake up, Joy. It's not your time."

"I'm dead, aren't I? That's why you're here."

My mother smiles, and in that one expression is my whole childhood, years and years of feeling safe and loved.

I'm crying. I know it even before she wipes my tears away. "Stacey is marrying my husband . . ."

"Shhh." She kisses my forehead and whispers, "Wake up, Joy. It's not your time."

I don't want to wake up. "No."

"Wake up, Joy. Now." It is her mother's voice, the one I only heard when I was in trouble, and I'm helpless to ignore it, even though I know that when I open my eyes, she'll be gone. She won't be beside me, holding my hand and kissing me. The Suave shampoo and menthol cigarette scent of her will be gone again. "I miss you, Mom."

With a gasp, I'm breathing again. The pain is back, sharp as a piece of glass, throbbing in my skull. The air around me is thick with smoke.

Slowly, I open my eyes. It's hard to see anything, hard to focus in the falling rain. The sky is gunmetal gray, swollen with clouds and smoke. Raindrops clatter on the fuselage of the demolished plane. In the distance, I can hear sirens and motors and voices and footsteps, but it is all far, far away.

I am deep in the woods, hidden. Huge ferns grow all around me. My shoe is hanging from a branch over my head. It bobs in the breeze.

It is amazing I didn't hit a tree.

I crawl to my knees, grabbing a nearby nurse log for support. When I finally stand, I am struck by a wave of nausea. The world careens sickenly, then rights itself. I focus on getting my shoe, putting it on, as if I can't be saved in bare feet.

When I finish, I look up. Across the smoky, debris- and plane-cluttered clearing, I can see the outline of emergency vehicles. A string of people is moving through another part of the dark forest. Their flashlight beams fan out like some giant, glowing cowcatcher in the smoke.

I can get there.

I take one painful, wobbling step, and then another and another. As I approach the edge of the clearing, I wait for them to see me. Any minute they'll rush to my aid and take me back to my real life.

To the empty house on Madrona Lane

where I'll spend the holidays alone, to the Volvo with the tree strapped on top. To the calendar that will tick off days to my sister's wedding and the birth of her child.

Don't go back.

Is that my mother's voice or the wind?

"No one knows I was on the plane." I say the words out loud for the first time, and at that, the voicing of it, I glimpse an opportunity.

No one will notice my absence until school starts.

I glance around the forest.

Behind me, the trees are thicker, closer together, but moonlight shows me a path between them. It is almost like a sign, that beam of light. Although I feel shaky, and more than a little light headed, I begin walking away from the crash site.

It isn't long before I see a break in the trees, and hear the distant roar of cars.

Somewhere up ahead is a road.

THREE

I walk slowly through this dark and ancient forest. My head still hurts, my vision is blurring, and this place is like nowhere I've ever seen. It is as if I'm journeying in another dimension. Before me, everything is a labyrinth of shadow and moonlit smoke. Spiderwebs connect it all together; in the uncertain light, the strands seem to be made of colored glass. Mist coats the ground, swallows my feet and the spongy earth.

At last, I come to the end of the woods and the start of civilization. It is a road, old and untended, and I turn to follow it. The dotted yellow line painted down its center is inconsistent, an afterthought, apparently, a suggestion rather than a law. Every few feet a yellow sign warns drivers to watch out for elk.

Every time I hear an approaching engine, I hide in the trees. I don't want some Good Samaritan to "rescue" me. It's mostly emergency vehicles, anyway, going too fast to see a lone woman who doesn't want to be seen.

At last I come to the edge of a town. A brightly painted sign welcomes me to the heart of the rainforest. The sign is splattered with mud and half hidden by a gargantuan fern, so I can't read the name of the town, but I see the word Washington.

I'm not in Canada.

"But I'm supposed to be in Hope," I say to the emptiness around me. Trees commiserate, whisper in understanding. They know how it feels to be uprooted, disappointed. It's bad enough that my one spontaneous decision in life leads to a plane crash; I could at least crash near my destination.

Then again, what difference does it make where I am?

I step out from the veil of trees and follow the ribbon of asphalt into town, smoothing my hair as I go. I have no idea how long I've been walking; this place seems too unreal to be tethered by something as scientific as time.

I should be wondering **where** I'm going, but I don't care. My mind is floating.

The town that isn't Hope looks like a movie set. Night tucks in around it; what's left glows in the light of street-lamps and holiday lighting. Santas and snowmen hang from lampposts; strands of white lights frame the windows.

The stores are closed for the day, and I'm glad. I don't want to see anyone yet.

What I want is a bed. My head is hurting again and I'm beginning to feel the cold. In a small, warm diner I find a wall of pamphlets and one old man drinking coffee at a bar. I see an adver-tisement for the Comfort Fishing Lodge, and a feeling of destiny settles around me, makes me shiver. It is the pretty little place I read about in **Hunting and Fishing News**. The place that welcomed me to come and stay awhile.

I could use some comfort. And I certainly need a place to stay.

I leave the light and heat of the restaurant and try to follow the map on the brochure.

I am alone again, and cold, and my head is really starting to hurt, but at least I have a destination.

I find Lakeshore Drive and follow it, walking along its crumbling edge, stepping over tire-sized potholes, for so long my feet start to ache. It begins to really bug me that I'm missing a sock. It's odd; my head hurts, my skin feels raw, my stomach is on fire where the seat belt bit me, I've walked away from an accident scene (that has to be illegal), and I'm worried about blisters on my feet.

It is quiet out here in a way I've never experienced; it's not the city way of silence, when folks are asleep and their cars are parked. This is a preternatural kind of quiet, where birdsong can startle you with its volume and a squirrel can be heard scampering up a tree as you approach.

I'm enough of a city girl to wonder what I'm doing in this no-man's land.

I find myself glancing back down the road, toward town, wishing I could hear a car. I'm just about to head back, in fact, when I turn the last corner and find myself in a large clearing, with a still, flat lake on my left and the immense forest on my right. The road becomes a driveway, lined on either side by bare-limbed fruit trees. At its end is a rustic—no, run down—log building. The roof is a carpet of moss. The wraparound porch sags tiredly to one side. To the left of the front door is a large chainsaw carving of a trumpeter swan. Beneath it is a hand-painted sign welcoming me to the

Comfort Fishing Lodge. Beside this sign is another—one that reminds me of my own life.

"For Sale."

Great. What do I do now?

I'm too tired to walk back to town. Some guy is playing drums in my head.

I will throw myself on the owner's mercy. Surely he'll have one room to rent. What choice do I have?

"No wonder I only dreamed about adventures," I mutter, following an untended stone path from the parking area to the lodge, where I find the front door ajar.

"Hello?" I call out, stepping inside. My greeting fades into the quiet, unanswered.

The lobby is a big room with a huge stone and timber fireplace and twin floor-to-ceiling windows that overlook the lake. Shadows cling to every surface, but in the moonlight I can make out a green-and-red plaid sofa that faces the fireplace, two worn red leather chairs, and an antique trunk serving as a coffee table. Black-and-white photographs, matted in white and framed in dark wood line the walls. Even from a distance, I can tell that the prints are antique.

To my right is a brass and wood registration desk, complete with an antique cash register. A display case in front of it is filled with brochures and flyers.

I stand there in the shadows, trying to figure out what to do, but it's difficult to think. My head hurts.

Maybe I should just lie down on the sofa and go to sleep.

But I'm desperate for a bath.

I've already committed a crime—breaking and entering—so I may as well find a bathroom and a bed.

I move forward cautiously.

One by one, I try to open the doors. None of the knobs turn for me, so I go upstairs. A single door is open to my left.

I creep cautiously forward, and step into the room. Everything is in shadows; it takes me a minute to focus.

When I do, I see a boy, sitting up in bed, rubbing his eyes and blinking at me. "Mommy?"

"No. I'm Joy. I'm sorry to just walk in on . . ."

"Are you real?"

I smile at that. "Yes. I'm trying to check in to the lodge, but there's no one at the desk."

"We're closed."

"Oh. Is there another motel nearby?"

Now my head is pounding

"Nope."

This has certainly been my day. "Great." This half-baked adventure of mine is going from bad to worse.

"We got rooms, though," he says tiredly. "And I know how to check guests in."

"Really? I need . . ." my voice cracks on that. There are too many things I need. It's best to focus on just the one. "A room for the night would be great."

"My dad won't like it, but this is my house, too." He throws back the covers and gets out of bed. Walking past me, he heads out into the hallway, and then looks back at me. "You coming?"

"Oh. Sure."

He leads me downstairs and shows me to the last door on the left side of the hallway. "Here." He twists the knob and opens the door.

Inside the room, I find a narrow dresser, a queen-sized bed, and a desk in the corner. In the shadowy darkness, everything looks shabby but clean. "Thank you," I say. "About paying . . ."

"People pay when they leave."

That's a relief. I can get my bank to wire funds at the end of my stay if I don't have enough cash.

"Maybe I'll see you tomorrow," he says, and then he's off, running for the stairs.

I close the door behind me, and there I am, caught by moonlight in the rectangular mirror above the dresser.

I look like hell. Leaves and twigs inhabit my red hair, which has somehow puffed up to three times its usual size. My blue eyes—usually my best feature—are bloodshot, and my pale, freckled skin is blotchy with dirt.

Something's wrong.

Blood.

Where is it?

I see scratches and scrapes but no deep wounds.

Thank God.

It must have been rain I tasted as I lay there. Maybe I bit my tongue . . . or maybe that metallic taste was tears.

It doesn't matter.

What matters are a bath and a bed. In that order. I open the small connecting door to my bathroom.

Shower. Not a bath. A shower. I'm disappointed but hardly surprised. This has not been a day when things went my way.

I step into a steaming hot shower with my clothes on.

Why not?

Everything needs to be washed.

The first part of my slumber is bad, I'll admit it—a kaleidoscope of ugly memories. The crash. My sister. Thom. The crash. But what I learn is this: when you're tired enough, you fall asleep, and nothing heals your mind like a peaceful night. When I waken, I feel remarkably good for a woman who survived a small plane crash and is currently running away from her real life.

No.

I'm not running away. I'm on my first adventure.

Still, I can't help hoping—just for a second—that Stacey is still at my house, waiting for me. Worrying. Maybe she'll think I've been kidnapped and call the police. **Then** she'd be sorry for sleeping with my husband and breaking my heart. But even as I dive into the warm fantasy, I feel it grow cold. She won't call the cops, won't mount a search. A year ago, she would have. Not now. She no longer knows my life well enough to wonder at my absence. For all she knows, I'm on the beach in Jamaica with some young hottie.

Or in a wild and primitive rain-forest . . .

I listen to the birds outside my window. I can hear the lake, too, lapping lazily against the shore. Somewhere a radio is playing.

In the bathroom, I find a small travel set in the top drawer. Toothbrush, tooth-paste, shampoo, and body lotion. It's everything I need. So I take another long, luxurious shower and dress in yes-terday's clothes. My black pants are dry, but stiff, likewise my now clean sweater set.

Showered and dressed, I feel ready to begin this adventure of mine.

I grab my camera and leave the safety of my room—1A, according to the plaque on the door—and go in search of someone to check me in. If I'm lucky, the boy is right and I can pay at the end of my stay.

The lobby is filled with pale sunlight and warmed by a crackling fire. In the light coming through the window, everything looks incredibly sharp and bright. Even the worn red-leather chairs and plaid sofa. I can see tiny diamond flecks in the fireplace's stonework. In contrast, without the sunlight, the registration area seems dull and vaguely gray. This is a part of the world where light changes everything, obviously. I take a few photographs of the lobby for my scrapbook, then turn toward the door.

In the distance, I hear the high pitched whine of a tool—chainsaw, maybe, or a weed eater. A few moments later, there are footsteps outside, coming up the walk, crossing the deck.

The door opens.

It's the boy I met last night. He's younger than I thought—maybe eight or nine years old—with shaggy black hair and freckled cheeks. His lashes are long enough to make him beautiful. But it is his eyes that I notice most. They're ice blue and sad.

When he sees me, he drops the hammer he is carrying.

I smile. "Hello again. It's nice to see you."

"Oh, boy." He crosses his arms. I recognize the body language. It's what I do now when I look at my ex-sister, cross my arms, as if a few more layers of muscle and bone can protect my heart. "I thought you'd be gone."

I hear the way his voice trembles; it's loneliness, that sound. The sense that your boat has come untied and you're drifting away. It's what I've felt everyday for almost a year. It's why I'm here, pretending I don't have a sister. "I'd like to stay awhile. If that's okay."

Before I can say more, the front door bangs open, and a man walks in. He is whipcord lean, with close-cropped black hair and a face that is all sharp lines and deep hollows. A dark stubble shadows his sunken cheeks; the harsh color accentuates the paleness of his skin. His eyes are strangely green, a color too bright for the rest of his hard, weather-beaten face. I can see how handsome he once was, before life wore him down. I know how he feels. Sometimes in the last year, I've thought that my color was washing away in the shower or fading in the sun. I wouldn't have been surprised to wake up one morning and find myself a black-and-white woman moving through a colored world. He doesn't even notice me. He is looking directly at the boy. "What are you doing in here, boyo? I thought we were cutting trees together?" His voice is deep and rich, softened by an Irish brogue.

"I came in for a Coke and found **her**."
He points at me. "Last night I checked her
in to room 1A . . . just like mom and me
used to do when this place was open.
Before **you** showed up."

The man looks at me for a second,
maybe less. I am of no interest to him,
obviously. "A guest, huh? Well, that's
grand." The way he says the last word
leaves no doubt about his reaction. He
does not find it grand at all. And though
his voice is full of sarcasm, a lilting Irish
brogue softens it. He barely looks at me.

"I guess my presence is a bit surprising," I say. "I'm sorry about that. I got
here late last night. I'd really like to stay
a few days."

The man bends down for the hammer. Even with the distance between us,
I can hear his sigh. "I know you don't
want me to sell this place, Bobby, but
one guest isn't gonna change things."

"You said you were selling cause no
one stayed here."

"That's **not** what I said."

"I love it here," the boy—Bobby—cries out. "And I know how to check in guests. Mommy taught me."

The man seems to deflate at that. "Aye."

"I won't be any trouble," I say. Suddenly I'm scared. If I leave here, I'll go home. I know me. I've never handled obstacles particularly well, and I don't want to go home yet. Stacey will be wait ing for me; I'll have to deal with the wedding and the baby and my broken heart. "Just a few days. Please? I need a vacation."

"She's stayin'," Bobby says defiantly, looking at his father.

The man looks at his son, and in the glance that goes between them, I see a pair of people who've lost their way together. "Tell her not to expect anything from me. I'm too busy to play host."

I feel a surge of gratitude. Every runaway needs a break, and this stranger has given it to me. I can stay here—hide out—for a while, just long enough to catch my breath and gather my courage for the next round of real life.

"I really appreciate this. You . . . can't know . . ." I don't know how to express it, how much this means to me. If I say all that I'm feeling he'll write me off as a wacko. "I'm Joy," I say by way of introduction.

"He's Daniel. I'm Bobby."

Daniel looks irritated. "Come on, Bobby, I need your help clearing trees down by the lake. Your mum let this place go."

Bobby moves reluctantly toward his father. When they are at the door, Bobby looks back at me. Then, wordlessly, he follows his father outside.

FOUR

*I*n the quiet that follows their departure, it strikes me: **I'm staying**. I am on my first vacation in years, and I am in an exotic location. Although it started off rocky (okay, so that's a mammoth understatement), as the kids at school say: it's all good now.

I have been given a great gift in this holiday season.

Time.

Time to let go of some of this baggage that has weighed me down in the past year. There's no way for me to gauge how long this interlude will last, so I better take full advantage of the time I have.

No whining or moping or crying. That's the resolution I make.

Here, for as long as my time lasts, I intend to be the old—or, perhaps the young—Joy Faith Candellaro, the woman who believes in love and marriage and fairy tales. The woman I used to be.

But first I need to find something to eat—I'm starving.

It takes me hardly any time to find the kitchen. The small, old-fashioned space reminds me vaguely of my mom's kitchen in the house in which I grew up—same yellow beadboard cabinets, silver appliances, and oak plank floors. It has a lovely, homey feel, and the scent of freshly made coffee makes my mouth water.

The coffee tastes better on my vacation than it ever did at home. Same goes for the bagel and cream cheese I find in the fridge. Opening the drawer by the stove, I look for a paper and pen. Like all junk drawers everywhere, it's full: playing cards, paper clips, store receipts, recipes ripped out of magazines, red marking pens, and travel brochures. Tucked in the back is a brand new DVD movie, unopened. **The Lost Boys.** The receipt taped to its face is dated three days ago.

It's the same movie I bought a week ago, on sale at Target.

So, we have the same weird taste in movies. Smiling at the unexpected connection, I find what I'm looking for: a notepad and pen. On the blue-lined page, I write: bagel, one tablespoon cream cheese, coffee. At the end of my stay, I'll figure out a way to pay for all of it. Thank God for the computerized world. It won't take five minutes at an ATM for me to get cash, even here, in the middle of nowhere.

Later, perhaps I'll take a cab to town, but for now, I want to explore this place where I have so unexpectedly landed. I stop by my room, get my camera, and go outside.

In full daylight, I am amazed by this wild, isolated corner of the world.

Everything is washed out, softened somehow by air that is threaded with fog. There is water everywhere: in the grass that springs beneath my feet, in the steady dripping of drops from branches and eaves, in the slap of waves against the dock. I feel rejuvenated by the moisture, like a desert traveler who has stumbled onto an impossible oasis. I can't see anything with perfect clarity; it is a world veiled by mist and water, and yet made all the more beautiful by obscurity. Lord knows I've seen my life too clearly in the past year. I choose my photographs carefully; I don't know when I'll get more film.

Looking for the perfect shot, I walk out toward the lake. The water is a soft gray, striated by reflections of the clouds above.

The shore is made up of tiny bits of pea gravel and stones that seem polished to a mirrored black sheen. A silvery wooded dock juts out above the water.

Waves slap playfully at the pilings. Not far away, a gorgeous hand-built swing set stands empty; every now and then the wind rattles the chains.

There are no other houses on the lake that I can see. It is almost primeval, this forest. I have never seen anything like it. I turn and look back at the lodge. From a distance, it looks more quaint than run down. According to the article I read, the place is more than sixty years old. In the photographs in the magazine, there were kids on the lawn, tossing Frisbees to one another and trying to use hula hoops, others playing badminton and croquet. No doubt the canoes and paddleboats and kayaks stacked by the dock would have been in constant use.

For the rest of the day, I poke through the cabins behind the lodge. They are shabby but quaint. With a new coat of paint, refinished floors, and a lot of scrubbing with bleach, they could be ready for guests. The old windows, with their wavy glass and clear maple trim, are in great shape, as are the skinned log interior walls.

I take pictures of all of it—of spiderwebs beaded with dew, of swans on the lake, of listing cabins furred by moss and inhabited by mice. All the while, I find myself imagining what this place **could** be. There was a time, ten or twelve years ago, when I dreamed of owning a bed and breakfast. During those years, I collected dozens of books and hundreds of articles on inn management. I can picture each cottage with old-fashioned brass beds, big fluffy down comforters, and hand-painted dressers.

Now, as I stand on the dock staring out at the lake, holding my camera, I think of the file cabinets in my garage, and the adventures-to-be within their slick gray metal sides.

I should never have let Thom relegate my dreams to the garage. That, I see now, was the beginning of the end. Even yesterday that realization would have made me cry; now I find myself smiling.

I'm dreaming again, for the first time in years, and it feels good.

A sound breaks my thoughts. I turn slowly, scan the place.

Daniel is on the roof, hammering shingles. There's a lonely sound in the way the nails ring out. I watch him for a long time, almost willing him to look up and see me, but he works like a machine or a man on a mission, without pause.

Finally, I turn away and walk along the shore, kicking rocks, noticing the moss that grows on everything. It's like being in the land that time forgot. Every leaf is huge, every tree towering, every stone coated with moss. I am about to reach down for an agate when I hear a child's voice.

"I don't know," the voice says, trembling. "Maybe."

I follow the sound into the woods and find Bobby, kneeling in a clearing. Evergreens ring him, rising high into the swollen sky, blocking out all but a single, golden shaft of light. The ground is a bed of lime-green moss and tiny fiddleback ferns. In front of him is a rustic wooden bench made of twisted and shiny tree limbs.

Bobby looks incredibly small in this spot, surrounded as he is by giant trees. "Not yet," he says to no one. "Don't go."

I can hear the tremor in his voice and it moves me, compels me to take a step closer. "Bobby?"

He stiffens at the sound of my voice, but doesn't turn to me or answer.

I move closer. Edging past him, I start to sit down on the bench.

"STOP!" he screams, pushing me aside. "You'll sit on her."

Something in his voice makes my blood run cold. I stop suddenly. "Bobby?"

He kneels in the dirt and slumps forward. "It's okay now. She's gone. You can sit."

He looks utterly broken, this boy who only yesterday defied his father to let me stay here. He picks up two action figures from the ground beside his knees and makes them battle. It's Darth Vader and Count Dooku, I think. A woman doesn't work in a high school without learning about popular culture. I finally sit down on the bench in front of him. "Are you okay, Bobby?"

"Fine."

"You don't sound fine. Do you want to tell me why?"

"You'll think I'm crazy, too."

"Why would I think that?"

He uses Darth to smack Dooku. "They all think I'm wacko."

"I doubt that."

He finally looks at me. "They don't believe I see her."

"See who?"

It takes him a moment to say, "My mom. She's dead."

I feel as if we've just swum out too far in cold water. "Is that who you were talking to when I got here?"

He nods. "I'm not crazy, though. I know she's in Heaven. But I see her sometimes. Dad thinks she's **imaginary,** like Mr. Patches."

"Mr. Patches was an imaginary friend of yours?"

Bobby makes a sound of disgust. "Uh. **Yeah.** When I was like . . . **four.**" He goes back to his action figures, makes them fight. "I'm **not** imagining my mom."

I find myself thinking of the plane crash, when I "saw" my mom. The vision was so complete and full, I believed it and I'm an adult. A boy this age could hardly be expected to fully comprehend tricks of the mind.

Of the heart.

"I saw my mom just the other day, and she's been dead for ten years."

Bobby looks up again. "Really?"

I nod. "I talk to her all the time."

Bobby seems to consider that, and me. "Does she talk back?"

I think about that. On a few memorable, rare occasions, I've felt her presence. "In a way, maybe. Mostly I think I know what she would say."

Bobby starts cracking the action figures together again. "He's glad she's dead."

"Who is?"

"My dad."

I glance out toward the lake and, though I can't see the lodge, I can hear Daniel hammering.

"Now I'm s'posed to pretend to like him."

"What do you mean?"

He shrugs. "Him and Mommy got divorced when I was four. I don't even know him. He's only here 'cuz she's dead."

Four. The same year Mr. Patches arrived. I've had enough child development classes to make the obvious connection.

I consider carefully how to respond. We are speaking of serious matters of the heart here, and it's hardly my place, but we teachers know that timing isn't always perfect with kids. If they bring up a sensitive subject, you'd best run with it. There is often no second chance. "He's here, isn't he?"

"Lucky me." Bobby wipes his eyes and turns away from me, obviously embarrassed by the display of emotion.

I remember how he feels. When I was eight, my own dad walked out on us. I waited years for him to return. I slide off the bench and kneel in front of Bobby. "It's okay to cry," I say softly.

"That's what grown-ups **say,** but it's not true. Arnie Holtzner says only babies cry. And now everyone calls me crybaby at school."

"Arnie Holtzner is a butthead who won't have friends for long."

Bobby looks shocked by that. A tiny, hesitant smile plucks at his mouth. "You called Arnie a bad word."

"I can think of worse than butthead, believe me."

Bobby stares at me for a moment, obviously trying not to smile. "You want to watch me play?"

"Sure," I say, finding it easy to smile. I almost laugh, in fact. Here, in this strange clearing, hundreds of miles from home, I feel both lost and somehow found. I lower my voice. I hunker down, get eye level with the action figures. "Come on, Vader, fight back."

That night, though I fall asleep easily, I wake up in a cold sweat, unable to draw an even breath. Memories of the crash won't let go of me. I would swear that the grit in my eyes is ash.

I try to fall back asleep, but it is impossible. My headache has returned, as has the pain in my chest. It's not real, I know, just the phantom ache of a broken heart. It's a pain I've lived with since the day I came home unexpectedly and found Stacey and Thom together. Throwing back the covers, I get out of bed and go to the window.

The first pink brush stroke of dawn sweeps across the black sky. I grab my camera, get dressed, and leave my room. Halfway to the lobby, I hear a voice: It's Daniel's soft, lilting brogue.

I peer around the corner.

He is at the window, staring out at the lake. His black hair is a tangled, untended mess.

Moving quietly, I edge around the corner and I see what he's looking at.

Bobby is out at the lake, alone, and gesturing wildly. Even from this distance, and through the murky, unreliable dawn light, I can see that no one is near him.

I see her sometimes.

"God help us," Daniel says in a broken voice.

I know he is praying, asking God for help. Still, the words are given to me. I feel a strange binding to them.

With a curse, he goes outside and walks down the path to the lake.

I move cautiously toward the window, but from here, I won't be able to hear them. If I'm going to eavesdrop, I should do it correctly. On this specious bit of logic, which I know is really only curiosity, I slip outside and step into the dark shadows cast by a Volkswagen-sized rhododendron.

"What the hell, Bobby? I thought we agreed about this," Daniel says.

"You can't stop me from talking to her."

"Maybe tomorrow we'll go see Father James. He—"

"Go back to being a stork broker. I don't want you here," Bobby says. Pushing past his dad, he runs back into the lodge. He is crying too hard to see me.

Daniel stands there a long time, looking out at the lake. There's a strange intimacy between us; I'm trapped by his presence. I can't move from my hiding place without risk.

At last, he turns away from the water and returns to the house, muttering under his breath as he passes me. Once inside, he slams the door shut so hard it bangs back open.

I stand there a long moment, in the darkness, then step out into the dawning light. Behind the black trees and gunmetal gray lake, the sky is awash in layers of color—fuschia, lavender, neon orange.

I bring the camera up and find the perfect shot, but by the time I take it, I've lost interest. What I care about right now can't be put in focus or framed in a neat little viewfinder.

Bobby and Daniel are in trouble. They are obviously drowning in a sea of what they've lost.

I know about those dark waters.

Someone needs to throw them a life ring.

FIVE

$\mathcal{B}$ack in the kitchen, I find a pot of coffee and a plate of muffins. Blueberry, my favorite. I add one cup of coffee and a single muffin to my tab, then go in search of mementos for my trip.

The perfect photograph. I'll accept nothing less.

Outside, the pink dawn has given way to a gray and yellow day of inconsistent weather: There, by the road, it's cloudy and rainy; here at the front door, it's shadowy and moist; down by the lake, it's sunny.

As I walk down the path, the air is thick with mist. Birdsong bursts forth in

Gatling gun spasms with every step I take. I snap several photographs before the swing set catches my eye. This is a magnificent specimen—obviously hand-built and carefully designed. It has a slide, two swings, and a fort.

I used to love swinging; at the house in Calabasas, Stacey and I spent hours in the air, side by side, and pushing each other. I go to the swing set, set my camera gently on a step, and wipe dew from one of the black leather seats. Sitting, I lean back and pump my legs until I'm practically flying. The lemon and charcoal sky fills my vision.

"Grown-ups don't play on the swings."

At Bobby's voice, I stab my feet into the loose dirt and skid to a stop.

He's standing near the skinned log stanchion. His eyes are bloodshot from crying. Tiny pink sleep lines crisscross his face. His curly hair is stick straight in places.

I feel an almost overwhelming urge to take him in my arms and hold him. Instead, I say: "They don't, huh? Who says?"

He frowns at me. "I dunno."

"You want to join me?"

He stares at me for a long time, then eases toward the other swing. There, he takes a seat and leans back.

"This is a great swing set. Someone worked hard on it."

"My dad made it. A long time ago."

Together we swing, side by side, up and down. The clouds overhead coalesce and disperse and float away.

"You see that cloud there?" I say, on the upswing. "The pointy one. What does it look like to you?"

Bobby is quiet for a while, then he says, "My mommy. She had puffy hair like that."

"I think it looks like . . . hmmmm. A Zipperumpa-zoo."

"A **what**?"

"You've never heard of Professor Wormbog and his search for the Zipperumpa-zoo?"

He shakes his head solemnly.

"Oh, my. I guess I'll have to tell you the story sometime."

"You promise?"

"Cross my heart."

He finally smiles and leans back, pumping his legs. "How about that cloud? It looks like a pointy stick."

"Or a piece of coconut cream pie."

He giggles. "Or Gandalf's hat."

We swing so long I go from feeling airy and light to light-headed. I slow down, stare out at the lake. Quiet settles in between us, turns awkward. "Maybe it's time for me to tell you that story now. We could sit on the grass."

Bobby sighs. "I gotta go to youth group today."

"Is that so bad?"

"Arnie Holtzner is there. And Father James always tries to talk to me about

Mom. He thinks I'd feel better if I prayed. As **if**."

I turn to look at him. "You don't think it would help?"

"God let her die, didn't he?"

"Ah," I say, recognizing the emotion. "So you're mad at Him."

Bobby shrugs. "I just don't wanna pray."

The clouds bunch up above us, take on a steely tinge. Before Bobby finishes saying, "It's gonna rain," it's pouring.

Laughing, we run for the house. Inside, I shake off, but no amount of movement will dry my clothes. I peel off my clammy sweater and wipe the rain from my eyes. "I have **got** to go to town for clothes."

"There's a lost and found box in your closet. My mommy kept **everything** in case people came back."

"Really?"

"Unless Dad threw it away. He can't wait to get rid of our stuff."

I hurry to my room, open the closet, and there it is: a cardboard box marked Lost and Found. The box is heaped with clothing of all kinds and sizes. After a thorough search, I choose a black broomstick skirt with an elastic waistband that falls almost to my ankles, an ivory boatneck sweater, and black knee socks.

When I return to the lobby, dressed in my new wardrobe, Bobby is waiting for me. "Can we play more?"

"I thought you had to go to youth group."

"Not till after lunch. Dad wants to finish painting the hall upstairs. So he can sell the place and move us to **Bawston**."

I can't help smiling at his perfect accent. I sit down on the floor beside him. "You don't like Boston?"

"I like it here."

"Have you told your dad that?"

"Like he listens."

"Maybe you should try talking to him."

Mondo hypocrisy. Suddenly I'm Dear Abby. Me, who ran away from a sister who wanted to talk. "My parents got divorced when I was about your age. My mom took my sister and me across the country for a new start. My dad just . . . let us go. I never saw him again."

"You're lucky."

I look at him. "You really think so?"

A frown darts across his forehead. For a second, I think he's going to say something. Instead, he gets up and walks over to the fireplace. On the hearth is an old wooden box; from which he produces two action figures. Gandalf in white with his staff and Samwise in full Orc regalia. "You wanna play?"

I can see how afraid he is to talk about his feelings for his father. How could I not understand that—me, who is on the run from real life?

I crane my neck, try to see into the box. "You have a Frodo in there?"

Bobby giggles. "Yeah. We'll pretend he's wearing the ring."

* * *

Bobby and I spend the morning on the living room floor, battling our way through Mordor and up the steep brick sides of Mount Doom. Honestly, I can't remember when I've had so much fun. We talk about things that don't matter and laugh about them. Sometime around noon, Daniel comes downstairs. Splattered with paint, carrying two brushes and a bucket, he walks past us. "Come on, Bobby. It's time for youth group."

"I don't wanna go."

"Too bad. Move it." Daniel opens the front door and sets his supplies on the deck. "Let's go, boyo. We'll have lunch at the diner first."

"C'n Joy . . ."

"No."

Bobby throws me a "**see**?" look and climbs to his feet. "I'm coming, Emperor."

It's all I can do not to smile at the tender defiance.

I would have called my dad a hell of a lot worse than emperor at his age. "Bye, you guys," I say from my place on the floor.

Bobby looks back at me longingly. "You can keep playing if you want. You can even be Frodo."

"I'll wait for you."

Daniel herds his son out the door. A few minutes later, I hear a car start up and drive away.

Then it's quiet again.

I try to figure out what to do next. I could walk to town for clothes and film and food, or take a walk in the woods, or borrow a canoe and go out on the lake, or sleep. Last night was hard: nightmares plagued me.

I close my eyes. It feels so great here, lying on the soft woolen carpet, feeling the heat from a fading fire, listening to the quiet.

In my dreams, I'm lying on an air mattress, floating on Lake Curran. The sun overhead is hot and bright; when I try to open my eyes, it hurts. I can feel people around me, splashing in the water. My sister's voice is the most constant: **I'm sorry**. The apology is repeated over and over. I know she wants me to open my eyes, take her hand, and tell her it's okay, but it's not okay. She's broken my heart. I hear my mother in my dreams, too, telling me to wake up. I'm sure that she wants me to forgive Stacey also. I want to tell them I can't do it, but then I'm floating away on the tide. I'm on the ocean now, alone . . . then I'm in a child's bed, then in a white room.

"Are you KIDDING me?"

The sentence shakes me, jars me. With great effort, I open my eyes. At first, I expect to see water, blue and lit by the sun.

I see green carpet and wooden planks and the lower half of a plaid sofa.

I'm in the lodge, asleep on the living room floor. I blink, trying to focus, and push up to my knees.

Daniel is in the registration area, pacing, talking on the phone. "What do you mean, a fight?"

I frown, sit back on my heels.

"He's eight years old," Daniel says, then curses under his breath. "Sorry, Father. And do you think I've not tried? God's the enemy now. And me."

I get slowly to my feet and stand there by the fireplace. He hasn't seen me yet, but when he does, I know he won't be happy. He doesn't want me in the lodge, let alone eavesdropping on personal conversations. But I can't seem to move. He looks so . . . the right word escapes me. Not angry, not upset.

Wounded.

"Aye," he says after a pause. Then, "I'll be right down." He slams the phone down on the table, then curses loudly and runs a hand through his hair. Slowly, he turns toward the living room.

I'm standing there, frozen, staring at him. "I'm sorry," I say, lifting my hands.

"Well if this isn't **just** what I need."

"I was on the floor. I didn't mean to eavesdrop."

His gaze slides past me—a pointed reminder that I don't belong here—and catches on the photographs on the mantel to my left.

Family photos.

With another curse, he storms out of the lodge and slams the door shut behind him.

Outside, I hear the car engine start, and wheels sputtering on wet gravel. Only then do I move.

I turn to the mantel, pick up one of the photographs. In it, Bobby is a pudgy-faced baby in a blue snowsuit. Daniel is smiling brightly and holding a beautiful, dark-haired woman close. There's no mistaking the love in their eyes.

No wonder Daniel is rude to me. This time is tough enough on him and Bobby without an uninvited spectator.

For the next half hour, I busy myself in the kitchen, making lunch and then cleaning up my mess. When I'm done, I return to my room, where I wash out my other clothes and hang them over the shower rod to dry, then I wander back to the lobby.

The fire is fading now, falling apart in a shower of sparks.

I am standing in front of it, warming my hands when they return.

Bobby comes in first, looking utterly dejected. "Hey, Joy. Dad says I can't play my GameBoy for two days. And I didn't start **nothin'**."

I turn to face them.

Daniel sits in the chair opposite me. I can tell by the way he looks at Bobby that he's been as bruised by this fight as his son. He doesn't look angry; rather, I see sadness in him. "This is a family matter," he says pointedly. "Don't talk to her. Talk to **me**."

Shut up, Joy.

Shut up.

I can't do it. Daniel's been out of his son's life for a few years; maybe he hasn't been around children in that time. "Kids get in fights," I say as gently as I can. "I'm a high school librarian. Believe me, I know."

"Not my dad," Bobby says, sidling up beside me.

"Not me what?" Daniel says, irritated. When he looks at us—Bobby and me—he's not smiling.

"You'd never get punched at school." Bobby's voice quivers. In the tremor, I hear how much he wants not to have disappointed his father.

To my surprise, Daniel smiles. "When I was a lad in Dublin, I got into plenty of scraps."

"Really?"

"Aye. And I got my arse kicked, I'll tell you. My own Da used to go after me. He said he didn't wanna raise no Mama's boy." His smile fades. "There's nothing wrong with bein' a mama's boy. She loved you something fierce, Bobby."

"I know."

"But she wouldn't want you fighting at church group."

"I know that."

I want to jump in with some stellar bit of advice that changes their lives and draws them together, but I know it's not my place.

For too long, we're all quiet.

Finally Daniel stands. "I'd best get to work on the bedrooms upstairs. No one is going to buy this place in the shape it's in. You coming?"

"I'm gonna show Joy my arrowheads."

Irritation flashes in Daniel's eyes and then is gone. "Fine. I'll work alone then." Without another glance, he goes up the stairs and disappears.

As soon as Daniel is gone, I look down at Bobby. "You aren't too nice to your dad."

"He isn't too nice to me." He pushes the hair from his eyes, revealing an angry purple bruise above his eye. "He yelled at me about fighting, and it wasn't even my fault."

I wish I could reach out for him, but he doesn't seem ready for comfort. So, instead, I say, "How does the other guy look?"

"I missed," Bobby says miserably. "And I wanted to hit him. I was so **mad**."

"What happened?"

His shoulders lump in defeat. "Arnie Holtzner punched me."

"The butthead? How come?"

" 'Cuz I'm a crybaby."

"You are no crybaby, Bobby. You're a very brave boy."

"Yeah."

"Tell me what happened."

"We were makin' Christmas ornaments out of cotton balls and Life Savers. I said I din't want to make one, and Arnie asked why, and I said 'cuz the ornaments were stupid and he said **I** was stupid and I said I wasn't. Then he socked me."

I want to say, **Arnie's an ass,** but I hold back. "Why didn't you want to make an ornament?"

" 'Cuz we aren't gonna have a tree."

His voice catches. He glances at the door his father just slammed. "My mom would **never** forget Christmas."

I know I should keep my mouth shut, but when I look down at this bruised little boy, I am drawn by some force that can't be denied. "You never know, Bobby. Christmas is full of magic."

For the remainder of the afternoon, Bobby and I play board games and watch Winnie-the-Pooh movies. All the while I can hear Daniel working upstairs— hammering, sanding, walking from room to room.

I tell myself to stay out of their business, but the admonition has a hollow, empty sound.

These two need help, and it's Christmas. I may have lost my own holiday spirit, but I can't watch a little boy lose his. Besides, this is my first real adventure. What kind of adventurer ignores the needs of others?

"Let's play again," Bobby says, reaching for his game piece.

I laugh. Three rounds of Candy Land are all any adult can reasonably be expected to survive, though, with Bobby drawing my cards and moving my game pieces, I must admit that I've hardly been paying attention. "No way. How about we do something else?"

"I know!" He pops to his feet and runs upstairs; moments later he's back, holding a mason jar full of rocks. "It's my collection." He flops down on the floor and dumps out the jar. Dozens of stones splatter out. Several arrowheads are mixed in with the pretty stones. Bits of beach glass add color to the pile.

I kneel beside him. "Wow."

He picks them up one by one; each piece has a story. There are agates, beach rocks, and arrowheads. His voice runs fast, like a weed eater in summer as he talks. **Mommy found this one by the river. This one was at the beach, hidden underneath a log. I found this one**

all by myself. When he's finished, he sits back on his heels. "She always said she'd find me a white arrowhead."

I hear the drop in his voice, the way grief sidles in beside him. "Your mom?"

"Yeah. She said we'd find it together."

To change the subject, I say, "What's that nickel doing in the jar?"

He barely looks at it. "Nothing."

There's definitely something in his nothing. "Really? No reason at all? Because those are your special things."

He reaches for a perfectly ordinary nickel. "Daddy gave me this when we were at the county fair. He bought me a snowcone and let me keep the change."

"And that blue button?"

It's a moment before Bobby answers, and when he does speak, his voice is soft. "That's from Daddy's work shirt. It came off when we were playin' helicopter. I . . ." He throws the nickel in the jar, then scoops everything back in. The arrowheads and rocks rattle and clang against the glass.

I smooth the hair from his forehead, but he is so intent on the nickel that he seems not to have noticed my touch. He looks as bruised on the inside right now as he is on the outside, and the sight of this poor kid, looking so lost, tears at my heart.

"How about if I read you a story?"

A smile breaks across his face. "Really?"

"Really. I don't suppose you have **Professor Wormbog and the Search for the Zipperumpa-Zoo**?"

"No, but I got one my mom always read to me."

I hear the tiny upward lilt in his voice, the single note of hope, and it makes me smile. "Go get it. And if you have a Dr. Seuss, get that, too."

Bobby runs upstairs. I hear his hurried footsteps overhead, the banging of doors.

In moments he is back, clattering down the stairs, clutching a pair of books. "I found 'em," he yells triumphantly, as if they were big game animals he'd bagged.

I sit down on the sofa and he curls up next to me, handing me a lovely blue book that is the Disney movie version of **Beauty and the Beast**.

I take it gently, open it between us, and begin to read aloud. "Once upon a time, in a faraway land, there was a magical kingdom where just about everything was perfect . . ."

The words take us to a place where plates and candelabras can be a boy's best friend and a beast can become a prince. I lose myself in the words, and find myself. In the past years, as my job became more and more about computers and technology and Internet searches, I'd forgotten why I started. The love of books, of reading. There's nothing a librarian likes better than sharing her love of words with a child. When I close the book, Bobby is beaming up at me. "Again!" he says, bouncing in his seat.

I put down **Beauty and the Beast** and pick up the bright orange Dr. Seuss. "Now it's your turn."

His face closes tighter than a submarine hatch. "I don't read."

"Come on." I open the book, point to the first sentence, and read: "I am Sam." Then I wait.

When the quiet stretches out too long, Bobby looks up at me. "What?"

"I'm waiting. It's your turn to read."

"Are you **deaf**? I can't read."

I frown. "How about just the first word?"

He glares at me, his chin jutted out. "No."

"Try. Just the first word."

"No."

"Please?"

I can feel his surrender. He goes limp beside me and sighs.

He stares down at the book, frowning, then says, "I. But that's just a letter. Big deal."

"It's also a word."

This time when he turns to me he looks scared. "I can't." His voice is a whisper. "Arnie says I'm stupid."

"You **can**. Don't be afraid. I'll help." I smile gently. "And you know what I think of Arnie."

Slowly, he tries to sound out the next word. When he stumbles, I offer a tiny bit of help and a heap of encouragement.

"S . . . A . . . M." Bobby frowns up at me. "Sam?"

"You read the whole page."

"It's a baby book," he says, but a smile plucks at his mouth.

"Babies can't read **I Am Sam**. Only big boys can do that." I turn the page.

By the time we get to **Green Eggs and Ham?** Bobby has stopped frowning. It takes a long time, but he finally sounds out the entire story, and when he finishes, he is laughing. "I read the whole book."

"You did really well," I say. Gently, I add, "Maybe you could read with your dad."

"No. I heard him tell my teacher that I needed a too-tor. That's something for dumb kids."

"A tutor is **not** something for dumb kids. I tutor kids in the library all the time."

"Really?"

Before I can answer, I hear footsteps coming down the stairs. Bobby and I both look up.

"Come on, boyo," Daniel says tiredly. "Let's go get some dinner in town."

"C'n Joy come?"

"No."

The curtness of Daniel's answer hurts my feelings—as ridiculous as that is—until I see his face. The question has wounded him. He is jealous of me—of Bobby choosing to be with me. I know a thing or two about jealousy, how it can cut you to the bone and bring out the worst in you. I also know that it is grounded in love.

"**Talk** to him," I whisper; the irony of my advice doesn't escape me. Apparently a woman running away from a conversation with her sister has no problem telling others to talk.

"Come on, Bobby. They run out of meatloaf early on weekends. And it's your favorite."

Bobby gets up. His shoulders droop sadly as he walks away from me. "No, it isn't. I like pizza."

Daniel winces. His voice tightens. "Let's go."

After they're gone, I sit on the sofa, listening to the dying fire. Rain hammers the roof and falls in silver beads down the windows, blurring the outside world. It is fitting, that obscurity, for right now, what I care about is in this lodge.

I have to do something to help Bobby and Daniel.

But what?

That night, I have trouble sleeping again. There are too many things on my mind. Sleep comes and goes; too often I am plagued by nightmare images of my sister and Thom, of the wedding invitation she handed me, of the plane crash.

But when dawn finally comes to my small, small room and taps on the window, I have only one worry left. The others I have let go.

Bobby's Christmas.

This is a problem I can solve, unlike the issues in my own life. Here and now, I can do something that will make a difference in someone's life, and perhaps that—the simple act of helping someone else—will help me in my own.

After a quick shower, I redress in my "new" clothes and head for the lobby.

As I suspected, Daniel is outside already. I can see him on his tractor, clearing the area down by the lake. Already, I know him well enough to know that he will work most of the day. Now is the time.

Running upstairs, I go straight to Bobby's room and find him still in bed. "Bobby? Wake up."

"Joy?"

"I have a plan."

He rubs his eyes. "What for?"

"A **secret** mission."

He sits up. "Like we're spies?"

"Exactly like that."

He throws back the covers and climbs out of bed. In his Spiderman jammies and clotted hair, he looks incredibly young.

"Downstairs," I say, checking my watch. "It's 9:07. You have five minutes or you'll miss the mission. Don't forget to brush your teeth."

He giggles.

I'm smiling, too, as I head for the door. Four minutes later, he comes barreling downstairs like a Saint Bernard puppy, all feet and exuberance.

"Did I make it?"

"Right on time. Now, Agent 001, we need to be quiet and careful."

He nods solemnly.

I lead him outside. We move cautiously, not wanting to be seen. Not that it matters. Daniel is deep in the trees now, out of our view.

We go to the spot where Daniel was working yesterday. There, at least a dozen young fir trees lay on their sides, waiting to be chopped into firewood. "Hmmm," I say, tapping my chin with my forefinger. "Which of these trees wants to come to your house for Christmas?"

Bobby gasps. "We're going to put up a Christmas tree?"

"We are."

"My dad won't like it."

"You let me worry about your father," I say with more bravado than I feel.

Bobby giggles again. "Okay, Secret Agent Joy . . ."

"Shh. You can't say my name out loud."

He clamps a hand over his mouth and points to a rather sad and scrawny tree, which he drags back to the lodge.

Once there, we move quickly and quietly. Bobby runs upstairs, then returns with a poinsettia-decorated red box full of lights. He makes this trip several times, until there are four boxes and a tree stand on the stone hearth.

It takes us almost twenty minutes to get the tree in the stand and positioned correctly. I am no help at all, which wouldn't surprise my sister. Bobby and I giggle at our ineptitude and hush each other. Every few minutes we go to the window and make sure that Daniel is busy. It isn't until I stand back to inspect the tree that I really **feel** it.

A tug of loss and longing. I can't help remembering how it used to be between me and Stacey at this magical time of year. Like the time she gave me the Holly Hobbie doll Santa had given her, just because I wanted it more. And there was the hellacious camping trip when we were little. Mom had been in full headband-wearing, tie-dyed T-shirt glory in those days. Singing and smoking and drinking through seven desert states. Stacey's sense of humor had kept me sane.

Now she'll be having Christmas morning without me. That's never happened before, not in the whole of our lives. I believe in reconciliation for Daniel and Bobby, but what about for me and Stacey?

"Why are you crying?"

I wipe my eyes and shrug. How can I possibly fold all that longing into something as small as words?

We pause for a moment, taking strength from each other, then we get to work. I decide to let him choose and place all the ornaments and lights. It's his tree, after all; my job is encouragement and understanding.

He goes to the box. Choosing takes a long time. Finally, he reaches down and finds an ornament. It is an intricately painted globe that reflects the rainforest. He shows it to me. "My mommy made this one."

"It's beautiful."

He puts the ornament on the tree, then returns to the box. For the next hour he moves in a ceaseless, circular pattern, from the box to the tree and back again. At each ornament, he says something, gives me some piece of himself.

Finally, he comes to the last ornament in the box. "This was her favorite. I made it in day care."

He hands it to me. I take it gently, mindful of the fragility of both its structure and sentiment. It is a macaroni and ribbon frame, painted silver. Inside is a photograph of Bobby and a beautiful dark-haired woman with sad eyes.

"That's her," he says.

Below the picture someone has written: Bobby and Maggie/2001.

"She's lovely," I say because there's nothing else. I wish he'd turn to me, let me hug him, but he stands stiffly beside me. Pushing the hair from his eyes, I let my hand linger on his warm cheek. "It'll get better, Bobby. I promise."

He nods, sniffs. I know he's heard those words before and doesn't believe them.

"She drove into a tree at night," he says. "It was raining. The day after Halloween."

So recently. No wonder he and Daniel are so wounded.

I wish I had something to say that would comfort him, but I've lost a parent. I know that only time will help him.

"I didn't say good-bye," he says. "I was mad 'cause she made me turn off **X-Men**."

My heart twists at that. Regret, I know, is a powerful remainder; it can bring the strongest man to his knees. One small boy is no match for it at all. No wonder he "sees" his mom.

He looks at me through watery eyes. Tears spike his lashes. The ugly purple bruise reminds me how broken he is on the inside. "I told her I hated her."

"She knows you were just mad."

"You won't leave me, will you?" he asks quietly.

For the first time I glimpse the danger I've walked in to. I'm a woman running away from trouble; that's hardly what this boy needs.

The silence between us seems to thicken; in it, I hear the distant sound of water slapping against the dock and the clock ticking. I can hear Bobby's sigh, too, as quiet as a bedtime kiss.

"I'm here for you now," I say at last.

He hears the word that matters: **now**.

"Bobby . . ."

"I get it. People leave." He turns away from me and stares at the Christmas tree. For both of us, I think, some of today's shine has been tarnished now.

People leave.

At eight, he already knows this sad truth.

The Christmas tree takes up the entire corner of the lobby, between the fireplace and the windows. Dozens of orna-ments adorn the scrawny limbs; there are so many the tree looks full and lush, even though they are oddly placed. It is, in every way, a tree decorated by a young boy. On the rough-hewn wooden mantel is a thick layer of white felt covered with glitter. Dozens of miniature houses and storefronts dot the "snow." Tiny street lamps and horse-drawn carriages and velvet-clad carolers line the imaginary streets. Bobby's favorite Christmas album—the Charlie Brown soundtrack—is playing on the stereo. Music floats through the speakers and drifts down the hallway.

He looks toward the window. "Is he coming?"

It is the fifth time he's asked me this question in five minutes. We are both nervous. An hour ago, it seemed like a good idea to decorate the house. Now, I'm not so sure. It seems . . . arrogant on my part, like the actions of a flighty relative who means to help and causes harm.

Last night, as I lay in my bed, spinning dreams of today to fight the nightmares of my real life, I imagined Daniel happy with my choice.

Now I see the naïveté of that.

He will be angry; I'm more and more certain of it. He won't want to be reminded of the past, or of his own carelessness with his son's holiday. He'll see me as an interloper, a problem-causer.

Bobby sits on the hearth, then stands. He goes to the window again. "How long has it been?"

"About thirty seconds."

"D'you think he'll be mad?"

"No," I say after too long a pause to be credible. Both of us hear my uncertainty. Bobby, who has been talking to a ghost for two months, seems attuned to the tiniest nuance of sound.

"He used to love Christmas. He said it was the best day of the year." He pauses. "Then Mommy and me moved out here and they got divorced." He goes to the window, stares out.

I can see his watery reflection in the window.

"He kept telling Mommy he was gonna visit me but he never did."

I have no idea what to say to that. I remember the day my own father left. I was just about Bobby's age, and I spent more than a decade waiting for a reunion that never came. My mom tried to ease my hurt with reassurances, but words fall short when you're listening for a knock at the door. Bobby knows about silence, how it leaves a mark on you. Then again, I know about divorce, too. It's possible that Bobby doesn't have the whole story. It's never one person's fault. The thought shocks me. It's the first time I've admitted it to myself. "The thing is," I say slowly, "he's here now. Maybe you should give him a chance."

Bobby doesn't answer.

Outside, a bright sun pushes through the clouds. The lake looks like a sheet of fiery glass.

"Here he comes!" Bobby runs to me, stands close.

The door opens.

Daniel walks into the lodge. He's wearing a pair of insulated coveralls, un-zipped to the waist. Dirty gloves hang from his back pocket. His black hair is a messy, curly mass; his green eyes look tired. "Hey, there," he says to us without smiling. He's halfway to the registration desk when he stops and turns toward the tree. "What have you done, boyo?"

I feel myself tensing up. It would be so easy for him to say the wrong thing now . . .

"We done it. Joy and me."

"Joy? Our house is her business now, is it?" he says quietly as he walks over to the tree.

Bobby glances worriedly at me.

We shouldn't have done it—I shouldn't have done it. That truth is bright and shiny now. I know nothing about them, not really. Sometimes memories hurt too much to be put on display. I am the grown-up here, the one who should have known better. I have to soften it for Bobby. "Daniel," I say, taking a step forward. "Surely . . ."

"You used all her favorite ornaments," Daniel says, slowly touching a white angel ornament.

"You bought her that one," Bobby says. "Remember? At the farmer's market by Nana and Papa's house."

Slowly, Daniel turns to face us. He looks still and stiff, like a man chiseled from granite. I wonder how he can bear it, the distance from his son. "Where's the star?" he asks at last.

Bobby glances at me. "It's on the table. We couldn't reach the top."

Daniel reaches down for the hammered tin star on the table. He is about to place it on the top of the tree; then he stops and turns to Bobby. "Maybe you and I can do it together?"

I hear the uncertainty in Daniel's voice, the fear that his son won't comply, and it reminds me how fragile we all are, how easily we can wound one another, especially when love is involved.

Stacey.

I close my eyes for just a second, awash in regret. When I open my eyes, Bobby is moving toward his father. The sight of them coming together makes me smile.

Daniel scoops Bobby into his arms and stands up. Daniel hands his son the star, and Bobby puts it on the tree.

They step back, admiring their work.

"It's grand," Daniel says. I hear a thickness in his voice.

"Tell Joy, Dad. It was her idea."

"I'm sure she knows I appreciate it."

"No. Tell her. She's right there."

Slowly, they turn to face me.

When Daniel looks at me, there's no mistaking the sheen in his green eyes. I can tell that he is a man who loves his son fiercely, maybe more than he knows how to bear. In that moment I forgive all his rudeness. Lord knows I understand how grief and love can break you. "Thank you, Joy."

"You could talk to her, Daddy. She's nice."

"I've not talked to women well in a long time. It doesn't come so easily anymore."

"It's okay," I say, feeling oddly connected to him. We are survivors of divorce, both of us; victims of a common war. Though I've been divorced for months, I hardly feel single. I feel . . . halved, or broken perhaps, and Daniel is right: conversation no longer comes as easily as it once did.

That's all it takes—the word, divorce— and I'm plunged back into reality. Suddenly I'm thinking of Stacey and Thom, of who we all used to be, then I'm thinking of the tree strapped to my Volvo, dying in the blackness of long-term parking.

"Joy, are you okay?"

Bobby's voice pulls me back. I smile at him, hoping it looks real. "I'm fine."

"Of course she's okay," Daniel says, "it's Christmastime. And now, as much as I'd love to chat with you and Joy, it's time for your doctor's appointment."

"Aw, **nuts,**" Bobby whines. "I don't wanna go."

"I know, boyo."

"Can Joy come? Please?" he pleads, looking from his father to me. "I'm scared."

"But **I'll** be with you, Bobby," he says.

"I need Joy."

I see how hurt Daniel is by that.

"I don't think it's a good idea," I say, studying Daniel's profile.

"Pleeease, Joy?" Bobby whines. Tears glaze his eyes.

I can't disappoint him. "Okay, but I'll stay in the waiting room."

Bobby wiggles out of his dad's arms and slides to the floor. "I gotta get Freddy."

As Bobby runs up the stairs, I stand there, staring at Daniel, who is looking now at the Christmas tree with an unvarnished sadness. I can see how much it has wounded him, this decorating of ours, and perhaps, his absence from it. I should say something, do something, but any word from me will be an intrusion.

And then my chance is gone. Daniel is moving past me, going up the stairs. Fifteen minutes later, he is back in the lobby, dressed in worn jeans and a forest green sweater. We leave the lodge and head for the truck. Bobby opens the door and climbs up into the cab, settling into the middle section of the bench seat. He is clutching a battered, well-loved stuffed lamb. I slide into place beside him. Daniel shuts the door and goes around to the driver's side.

The drive to town takes no time at all, but even in the mile and a half or so between there and here, I am blown away by the beauty of this place. Giant evergreen trees grow everywhere—along the roadsides, in great, dark forests that block the path to the snow-covered mountains in the distance.

"It's beautiful out here," I say, seeing the ghostly image of my own face in the window glass; behind it, all around me, are the green and black blur of the trees we pass.

The town is exactly as I remember it: a few blocks of quaint storefronts, draped in holiday garb. Traffic is stopped here by signs and pedestrians; there are no traffic lights. On this bright blue afternoon the sidewalks are busy. Everywhere I look, pods of people are gathered to talk. It looks like a Hallmark card until we turn a corner.

Here, the street is overrun with people and vans.

"Damn it," Daniel says, slamming on the brakes. "This is getting old."

I am just about to ask what's going on when I see the letters painted on the side of the van beside me.

KING TV.

It's the media.

The crash.

Of course. I turn my face away from the window instinctively. I know they aren't looking for me—can't be—but, it's better to be safe than sorry. Still, I catch a glimpse of the police station and the crowd clamoring at the door.

Daniel turns onto another road and we are in the clear. He maneuvers the old truck into a parking spot and kills the engine, which slowly sputters and dies.

In the silence that follows, Bobby looks up at his dad. "How come I gotta see the doctor again?"

Daniel unhooks Bobby's seat belt. "You've had some hard knocks, boyo. Anyone would be sad after losing their mum."

Bobby sighs and crosses his arms. There's a wealth of emotion in the sound. "But not everyone talks to her ghost."

Daniel sighs. "I'm tryin' to help, Bobby."

"It would **help** if you believed me,"

Bobby says. Slithering out of the cab, he runs on ahead.

I walk across the parking lot with Daniel. We are so close our arms are nearly touching, but neither of us pulls away. For a moment, as we enter the building, I imagine we're a family, the three of us, here for Bobby's regular checkup. If it were true, I'd follow them down the hallway and turn into the doctor's office. I'd answer all the doctor's questions about my son's health. No doubt the three of us would go for ice-cream cones when it was over.

Instead, I go to the waiting room and sit down, alone. At some point, while I'm staring out the window at a rhododendron the size of a luxury car, a nurse comes up to me. She puts a hand on my shoulder and peers down at me.

The touch startles me. I hadn't even heard her approach.

"How are we today?" she asks.

I frown. Had I fallen asleep? Had some kind of nightmare? I don't think so.

I was staring out the window, thinking about the big green leaves on the rhodo-dendron; that's all. I open my mouth to say "I'm fine, thanks," but what comes out is, "I'm alone."

The nurse with the plump, apple cheeks smiles sadly. "You're not alone."

It makes me feel better, that assurance, but when she leaves, I am alone again. Waiting.

For the first time since I ran away from Bakersfield and the crash, I wonder what it is I'm waiting for.

SIX

After the doctor's appointment, as we're heading across the parking lot, Daniel says, "I could go for some ice cream right about now. How about you?"

"Yippee!" Bobby squeals, bouncing with each step.

"Ice cream sounds good," I say, trying not to smile. It is the first time I've felt welcomed by Daniel, included.

Beyond the parking lot is a lovely tree-lined street with small, well-tended houses on either side. The yards are full of color, even on this chilly December day—bright green grass, yellow bushes, blue-green kale in terra cotta pots. Ornamental cherry trees line the sidewalk, and though the limbs are bare now, it's easy to imagine them awash in pink blossoms. Come spring, this street must look like a parade route with the air full of floating pink confetti.

As we reach the corner, we merge into the crowd out Christmas shopping on this sunny day. All around us, people are talking to one another. Every person we pass calls out a greeting to Daniel and Bobby.

We duck into a cute little ice-cream shop that proudly offers seven flavors. Behind the counter, a television is playing. On it, Jimmy Stewart is running down the snowy streets of Bedford Falls. The girl serving ice cream—a pretty teenager with a pierced nose and jet black hair—smiles at us. "Hey, Bobby. You want your regular?"

Bobby grins. "You bet. Double scoop."

The girl looks at Daniel. Her blush and stammer reminds me how good-looking he is. Even a teenage girl notices. "I'll have a pralines and cream," he says

in that velvet brogue that makes the girl
smile.

I am just about to order a single scoop
of cookie dough ice cream on a sugar cone
when a picture of a crashed plane fills the
television. On-screen, a local broadcaster is
standing in front of the charred wreckage,
saying, " . . . plane crashed in the woods
northeast of here. Survivors have been airlifted to several local hospitals for treatment. Authorities are in the process of
identifying survivors and contacting family
members. All of the named passengers on
the manifest have been accounted for."
Thank God. Everyone survived.

"However, witnesses report that an
unidentified woman bought a last-
minute ticket on the flight . . ."

Panic seizes hold of me. They're trying
to find me. Without thinking, I mumble,
"excuse me," and push past Daniel and
Bobby. I can't get out of here fast enough.

Outside, I collapse onto a park bench
and lean back. My heart is beating a mile
a minute.

I look up just in time to see Daniel and Bobby come out of the ice-cream shop. Both are frowning.

"Are you okay?" Bobby asks me.

I can see it in his eyes, the fear and worry. He is a boy who knows how life can turn on a dime, how people can be there one day and gone the next.

"I'm fine," I say, but I'm not. I'm not even in fine's neighborhood.

They're searching for me.

What do I do now? How much longer do I have in anonymity?

My purse. They could find my purse.

"What is it?" Daniel asks, looking down at us.

I'm panicked and shaky. I want to say **I can't go back,** but the words would make no sense to him. When I look up, I catch Daniel's gaze and lose my place. Something about the way he's looking at me makes my heart speed up.

"Is everything okay?" he asks.

His concern touches a place deep inside me. I have been alone—lonely—for too long. Apparently the slimmest strand of caring surprises me. I am stunned by how much I suddenly want to stay here. And yet, now I know that the clock is ticking. Once they discover my name, I will have to return home.

"I'm fine. Really."

I get to my feet, feeling unsteady. Bobby sidles up close to me.

Together, the three of us walk down the crowded street. The decorated windows catch my attention, give me something to think about beside the news story. Occasionally, we go into stores, and when we do, we are welcomed. People look at us and smile and wish us a Merry Christmas. Dozens of knickknacks and souvenirs tempt me; an ornament made of Mount St. Helens' ash, a wind chime made of copper and shells, a T-shirt that reads: "Wet and wild in the rainforest," but I don't have any money with me. I make a mental note to come back to some of these shops on my way out of town. I'll want to add plenty of brochures and flyers and maps to my file cabinets back home.

Back home.

I push the thought aside and focus on enjoying the day.

We stroll pass a diner with a Christmas painting on the window, then a frame shop.

Bobby stops dead.

I glance down at him. "Bobby?"

He's staring at the building to our right. It's a gorgeous stone church with stained glass windows, a big oak door, and a nativity scene in the yard.

Daniel looks down at his son. "We could go in and light a candle for your mum."

Bobby shakes his head, juts out his chin in a telling way. He isn't going to move.

"Maybe Christmas Eve," Daniel says gently, taking hold of his son's hand.

For the next half hour, we window-shop on Main Street, and then Daniel buys a bucket of fried chicken and we sit at a picnic table in the park to eat. Bobby sets out a paper plate, napkins, and a fork for me, but to be honest, I'm not hungry. The news story has ruined my appetite. Apparently I'm not the only one who has been upset by our little trip to town.

"So, Bobby," Daniel finally says, snapping open a Coke. "You want to talk about it?"

Bobby stares down at his plate. "Talk about what?"

"You being mad at God."

He shrugs.

Daniel studies his son. In that one look, I see a world of emotion; a man who knows how to love. "I'd take you, you know."

Bobby looks up at his dad, then at me. "I need Joy."

"We all could go to church," I say quickly, but it's too late. The damage has been done. Bobby has chosen me over his father again. I have to do something fast to change the mood. Somehow, I have to get these two to remember who they are to each other and what they have left. Sometimes that's all that matters: what remains. "Tell me about the time you and your dad went to the carnival."

"The time he le-let me keep the change?" Bobby asks.

I nod. "That time."

Bobby glances at his dad. "You remember that, Daddy? When we went to the carnival?"

That's all it takes—a word from Bobby—and Daniel's face changes. His smile takes my breath away. "Aye. At the county fair, it was. I'm surprised you remember that."

"You carried me on your shoulders."

"You spilled juice in my hair."

Bobby giggles at that. "Mommy said you looked like an alien with purple on your face."

Daniel's gaze is as soft as velvet, yet it hits me hard. I've never seen a man who looks at his son with such unabashed love. Once Bobby sees that, he'll know

he's safe in this world. "You were too little to get on the bumper cars."

"You said they were a dumb ride
anyway."

"Aye. And so they were."

For the rest of the meal, they trade
memories and stories. By the time we
head back to the truck, they are smiling
at each other.

On the way home, we listen to the
radio. It's Randy Travis's whiskey-velvet
voice singing "I'm Gonna Love You
Forever and Ever." As the words float
through the cab, I find myself looking at
Daniel.

When we get back to the lodge, it's almost seven o'clock. Bobby immediately
runs to the television and puts a DVD in
the machine. He's chosen **The Santa
Clause**.

I start for my room.

"Where you going, Joy?" Bobby says.

"You and your dad need some time together. I'll see you to . . ."

"No." He turns to Daniel. "Tell her, Daddy. Invite her to watch the movie with us."

I draw in a breath, waiting. I know he will release me and keep Bobby to himself. It's not even the wrong thing to do.

"Please," Daniel says softly, smiling my way. "Stay with us."

It isn't until then, when I hear his velvety brogue wrap around those three small words, that I realize how much I wanted Daniel to ask me to stay.

"Sure," I say, hoping I don't sound as desperate as I feel.

Daniel and Bobby sit on the couch together. I curl into the red chair, opposite them.

As I sit here, listening to Bobby's laughter, I consider how quiet my own house has become. If I'm to be honest—and why would I lie now?—our house was quiet long before Thom left me. Before he started sleeping with my sister. When I look back on my marriage, the truth is that it was too quiet from the beginning.

On that last night in Bakersfield, Stacey was right. My marriage had been falling apart long before she came into the picture. It's a truth I can finally admit.

"He's getting fat 'cuz he's Santa!" Bobby yells, bouncing in his seat.

His happiness is infectious; in no time, Daniel and I are laughing with him.

When the movie is over and Daniel says, "Time for bed, boyo," and Bobby grumbles and whines that he's not tired—even though he can't keep his eyes open—I am sorry to see the evening end, sorry to face the prospect of going back to my room.

Daniel picks Bobby up and carries him toward the stairs.

" 'Night, Joy," Bobby calls out sleepily. "See you in the morning."

"Good night, Bobby."

I mean to get up and go to my room.

I really do, but somehow I don't move. I sit there, curled like a cat in the chair, staring at the fire. The family photographs on the mantel seize my attention. I go to the mantel, pick up the pictures, and pour over them like an archeologist looking for clues from the artifacts of a life. Who was Maggie? Why did their marriage end?

Later, when I hear Daniel's footsteps on the stairs, I realize I've been waiting for him.

He comes into the room, stands in front of the fire. In the combination of orange light and dark shadows, he looks drawn and tired. We are close enough that a movement either way and we'd be touching. "I promised Bobby I'd come back down. I'm supposed to talk to you, don't you know?"

"I'm glad," I dare to answer.

"I'm not much of a talker these days." His voice is so soft I have to lean toward him to hear. "The funny thing is, I used to be a real loudmouth, back in the pubs in Dublin, when I was a lad. I could talk till I was blue in the face and falling-down drunk."

"It's funny how things slip away, pieces of us, even."

Daniel sighs. Nodding, he reaches for the single photograph left on the mantel, tucked now behind the Christmas village, and holds it close. It's a picture of Maggie, looking young and vibrant and beautiful.

I have no idea what to say or do. He looks so raw right now, so utterly broken, that I'm afraid to speak.

He puts the photograph back and sits down on the hearth. "So, Joy." He makes a sound that's almost a laugh. "Maybe you could help me, too. It seems I was a bad father and a worse husband. I didn't even **think** about putting up a Christmas tree. All I thought about was getting Bobby out of this place where the memories are so bad."

"Moving won't put his heart back together." This is a truth I know; I learned

it firsthand. I sit in the chair opposite
him and lean forward. In a daring that's
completely foreign to me, I touch his
thigh. "He needs **you** for that."

A frown darts across his forehead.
"What the hell . . ."

I draw back, instantly contrite. "I'm
sorry."

He gets to his feet. "The doc said I
should talk to you, for Bobby, but . . ."

I get up and go to him, unable to stop
myself.

We're close now, almost face to face. I
feel the softness of his breathing, smell
the hint of wood smoke scent that clings
to his T-shirt. "Daniel?"

"I feel like a bloody fool. How in the
hell am I supposed to talk to you?"

I step back. "I'm sorry. I shouldn't
have . . ."

What? Touched him? Said anything?
Come here in the first place? I have no
idea what to say to him, what I did that
was so wrong.

He turns away from me and goes to

the fireplace. When he's put out the fire, he goes about the business of closing up the lobby for the night, locking the doors and drawing the curtains shut, until the lobby is jet black. He disappears down the hallway, then returns.

I wait for him to look at me, and try to figure out what I'll say when he does. How I'll explain being an idiot for a second, a woman caught and blinded by her own needs. I try to make out his face in the dark. Is he smiling? Frowning? I can't tell.

When everything is dark and quiet he goes toward the stairs. I can hear his hushed footsteps on the carpet and the cadence of his breathing. I wait for him to pause on the stairs, to say **something,** but in this I am disappointed. He makes his way up the stairs; later, I hear a door open and close, and then I am left alone, standing by the fire, staring at the photographs of another woman's family.

*   *   *

The plane is going down.

"It's burning . . . don't touch . . ."

"Run!"

Too late.

I'm in the air, tumbling, screaming . . . we're going down . . .

I wake up, screaming in the dark of my room. My chest is crushed, my face smashed. I can't make my legs move.

I'm paralyzed.

No. I'm dreaming.

I touch my chest, press the skin until I can feel my heart beating. It's fast but steady.

"You're fine." The sound of my voice calms me, coming as it does from the darkness of my room. On shaking, weak legs, I walk to the window, push it open. The pine-scented air caresses my cheeks, grounds me instantly.

I'm here. Alive.

Tiny raindrops flutter on my face and the windowsill, cooling my skin. Gradually, I feel myself calming down.

The images fade, slink back into my subconscious.

I stand there, watching the shiny combination of rain and moonlight until my hands stop shaking and I can breathe evenly again.

I hear footsteps upstairs, pacing. Someone else can't sleep. Daniel.

I wish I could go to him, say simply, "I can't sleep, either."

Instead, I turn away from the window and return to my thin, empty bed.

Mist, as translucent and flimsy as a layer of silk organza, floats across my window, blurring the forest beyond. Everything is obscured by the haze; two-hundred-foot trees appear strangely fragile. Even time seems elastic; the days and nights are passing with near impossible speed. I know that it is because I want time to slow down that it is speeding up.

This morning, as I stand at my window and look across the yard, I see shadows moving in and out among the trees. It doesn't surprise me that Bobby sees his mother in all this softness. There is an otherworldliness to the forest here. I also know how easy it is to see what you want to see.

For almost the entire year before Thom betrayed and left me, I knew he was unhappy. I was unhappy. But we did what people do—we closed our eyes and thought it meant we didn't see.

I knew he was talking to Stacey about our troubles.

If I'd **looked** instead of merely seen, I wouldn't have been so surprised by how it ended.

This is my resolution for the New Year. I will be honest with myself. I'll keep my eyes open. I'll see what's there, not just what I want to see.

After my shower, I redress in my old clothes and get my camera.

The lobby is quiet, steeped in tea-colored shadows.

I walk past the cold dark fireplace.

Daniel's truck is gone. No wonder the place is so quiet.

Peaceful.

That's what the quiet is here. Unlike in my home, where for the last year the silence has been like the indrawn breath before a scream.

The quiet and the mist draw me outside. I stand in the yard and stare at the silvery lake beyond. Through the haze, the dock looks almost translucent, a charcoal line against the gray-tipped waves.

I need a photograph of this. Maybe several.

I lift the camera to my face and work to put a blurry world into focus. It's not until I've taken several shots that I realize how cold I am. Disappointed, I return to the warmth of the house. But I feel the need to walk in that pearlescent mist.

I could borrow a coat.

Why not? I checked myself in; I eat their food. I'm certainly making myself at home. Besides, they're gone. I'm sure neither would begrudge me the use of a jacket for an hour or two.

It takes some searching, but I finally find a coat closet near the back door. In it is a jumble of coats and sweaters and yellow slickers. I pull out a bulky, beautifully knit aqua-blue fisherman's sweater and slip it on. It's huge on me, but warm.

For the rest of the day, I explore this magnificent corner of paradise and take seventeen photographs—of the sunlight on the lake, of a swan taking flight, of a spiderweb turned into a necklace by dew drops. By mid-afternoon, I have begun to imagine how I will frame these prints and display them.

In my living room, I think, above the sofa. Every day of my real life, I will look up and remember this adventure. Finally, at around two o'clock, hunger sends me back inside.

I am just finishing a sandwich when I

hear the truck drive up. Quickly I clean up my mess and run to the living room to greet them. It's silly, I know, perhaps even stupid, but I don't care. I've missed them today.

Bobby rushes in. "Joy!"

I love the way he says my name; it's as if he's been missing me all day. "Hey, Bobby," I say, looking behind him for Daniel, who comes in a moment later, looking so handsome that I catch my breath.

Bobby runs at me. "It's beach night."

"We need to leave in about fifteen minutes," Daniel says. "So you'd best hurry up."

He is looking at me. A shiver runs up my spine. "I'm invited?"

Bobby giggles. "'Course."

"Get a coat," Daniel says to both of us. "It's cold out there."

I decide to move fast, just in case Daniel wants to change his mind. Feeling like a girl on her first date, I run back to my room and retrieve the big cable knit sweater. It's certain to be warm enough.

In two minutes, I'm back in the lobby with Bobby.

"Did you brush your teeth?" Daniel asks his son.

We both answer, "Yes," at the same time.

At the sound of our laughter, Daniel smiles, and I am blown away by the sight of it. It takes ten years off his face and gives me a glimpse of the hell-raiser of the Dublin pubs. "Come on, then." He slings a backpack over his shoulder and leaves the house. Bobby and I follow along behind him, still laughing. It is the freest I've felt in years, and I wonder what it is about this place and these people. Here, with them, I become so easily the younger version of myself, the me I always imagined growing into. I'm more like my mother—free, loving, easygoing. In the dry, dusty town of Bakersfield I'd been a flower slowly dying; in the moisture and mist of this green cathedral, I can feel myself blossoming.

In the truck, we turn up the radio and sing along to Bruce Springsteen. "Baby, I was born to run" are suddenly the most meaningful words I've ever sung. By the time the song is finished, we are on an old, winding, two-lane highway. For miles, we are surrounded by trees, then we come to the harvested part of this great forest. Acres of shorn land lie on either side of the road. All that's left are tiny new plantings and signs that talk of reforestation and regeneration.

"It's sad," I say. "As if new trees are no different than old ones."

Bobby tilts his face to look at me. "What do you mean?"

"You live in one of the few old growth forests left on the planet. Cutting down trees that have lived for two hundred years is a crime."

"Will they go to jail?" he asks.

"Who?" Daniel says, hitting his turn signal and easing to a stop.

"The loggers who cut down the old trees."

"Oh. No," Daniel answers, frowning as he turns onto another road.

"It's not **literally** a crime," I say. "It's just sad."

"When I'm big, I'm gonna protect the old trees," Bobby says, nodding as if it's a stern, implacable decision.

"What started this conversation?" Daniel asks.

I'm about to answer when we turn a corner and park.

There it is, in front of us: the Pacific Ocean.

The huge, roaring expanse of blue water and gray sky is nothing like my familiar Southern California coastline, with its powdery sand and rolling surf and volleyball nets placed every one hundred yards or so.

Here, the beach is as wild as the forest, as primitive, too. Waves crash onto the shore, sounding like a lion's roar, even from the distance of our car.

"Wow," I say, sitting back.

"Dad's never done beach night before

either," Bobby says. "Mommy and me did it every Tuesday night, after t-ball."

"I'm glad to be here," Daniel says. I can't tell if it's wistfulness in his voice or regret, or if he's missing his ex-wife. "How about your Joy? Is she a beach gal?"

Bobby turns to me. "Well?"

"I love the beach," I answer, looking at Daniel's profile.

"I knew it," Bobby says, bouncing in his seat. "She **loves** the beach."

I feel lit up inside. I don't know how else to put it. Daniel grabs his backpack and helps Bobby out of the car. The boy immediately runs on ahead, across the sand.

"Not too close to the water, boyo," Daniel calls out.

I slip into place beside him.

The beach is beautiful. A full, fiery sun hangs in the teal blue sky. Golden streamers light the waves. I have never seen so much driftwood on a beach before, and it is no ordinary collection of sticks. It is a heaping, jumbled mass of silvery logs, shorn of branches and polished to white perfection. Many of them are more than one hundred feet in length. The trees along the road have been sculpted by the wind. They look like giant bonsai.

"Dad, my kite!" Bobby yells, running back at us.

"Just a second," Daniel answers, bending down to make a fire. Within moments, the small circle of wood and newspaper is aflame. I sit on a log by the fire, watching Daniel teach his son to fly a kite. By the time Bobby gets it, the afternoon is fading. Neon orange clouds streak across a midnight blue sky.

"Look, Dad! Look, Joy! I'm flyin' it!"

"That you are. Run faster," Daniel says, laughing as he sits down beside me. He's so close I can feel the warmth of him beside me.

"I wish I'd brought my camera," I say.

Bobby runs toward us, dragging the kite behind him. It flaps against the heavy sand. "Didja see me?"

"I did," I say. "It's the best kite flying I've ever seen."

His smile is so bright it lights his dark eyes. He flops to sit on the sand beside us. Gradually, though, his smile fades.

Silence falls, broken only by the crackling of the fire and the whooshing of the waves.

"Have you got something on your mind, boyo?" Daniel asks.

Bobby kicks at the sand before he finally looks up. "How will we have beach night in Boston?"

"Ah. So that's what you're thinking about. Moving."

Bobby glances quickly at me. I nod encouragingly. He takes a deep breath and says: "I want to stay here, Dad."

"I know you do, Bobby."

"You were the one who picked it."

"Aye. Things were different then."

At that, the reminder of how their lives have changed, they fall silent. After a long pause, Bobby says, "Tell Joy how you found this place."

Daniel's sigh threads the night, falls toward me. I'm pretty certain it's a story he doesn't want to tell. He leans forward, rests his elbows on his thighs. Shadows and firelight mark his face. "We were livin' in Boston, in a house not two doors down from Nana and Papa. Your mom managed the makeup counter at Macy's and I spent my days—and too many nights—on the thirtieth floor of the Beekman Building. I used to dream of towering trees and lakes that were full of fish. Mostly I dreamed of us being together all the time, instead of all going our separate ways. One day I read about this summer house for sale in Washington State. It was a bed and breakfast that had gone bankrupt."

"And we bought it. Just like that," Bobby says, "Without seeing it even."

"Aye," Daniel says, and this time I'm sure it's wistfulness I hear in his voice. "We had our dreams, didn't we?"

"Yeah."

In the silence that follows, I know

they're thinking about how far apart they
are. All I can see is how close they've become. It will only take the merest move
by either one of them to find the middle
ground.

I twist around to face Daniel. We are
so close now. I can see the tiny grains of
sand and bits of ash that cling to his skin
and hair. His green eyes look at me with
an unnerving intensity. Behind me, I
know Bobby is watching us. "I can see
why you fell in love with this place. It's
magical."

"That's what Mommy always said." I
can hear the sadness in Bobby's voice.
"**Why**?" he asks suddenly. "Why do we
have to move?"

Daniel looks down at his hands, as if
he'll find the answer in his flesh and
bone. "I want the best for you, Bobby."

"This **is** the best."

Daniel looks at his son. "How am I
supposed to run this place all by myself? I don't know anything about fishin'
or such."

This is a question I can answer. "There are dozens of books that can teach you. I've read a lot of them. If you take me to the local library, I'll help you find them."

"Mommy tole me you were smart," Bobby says accusingly.

Daniel smiles at that. "I like to think so."

"Then **learn,**" Bobby says.

"I'll tell you what," Daniel says finally. "I'll think about staying if you'll think about leaving."

They look at each other, father and son, and in the fading sunlight and firelight, I am struck by how alike they are.

"Okay," Bobby says solemnly.

"Okay," Daniel agrees. "Now, how about some hot dogs and marshmallows before the sun leaves us for good?"

For the next hour, as the sun slowly drops from the sky and the stars creep into the night, we roast hot dogs and make smores and walk along the darkened waterline. I am too full from my late lunch to eat anything, but a lack of appetite doesn't keep me from enjoying the fire. A battery-operated radio, perched on a log behind the fire, cranks out one pretty song after another. Often, we sing along. Daniel's voice is pure and true and sometimes renders me voiceless. We are packed up and ready to leave when a beautiful rendition of "The Way You Look Tonight" starts.

By the way Daniel sings along, the harshness of his voice, I know the song means something to him.

"You used to sing this song," Bobby says.

"Aye."

"Dance with Joy."

I catch my breath, surprised.

"I don't think so," Daniel says, careful not to look at me.

"Pleeease," Bobby says, looking at us. "For me?"

I am in the darkness just beyond the dying fire's glow. Daniel is across from me. His face is all shadows and orange light. I can't see his eyes, but I know he's not smiling.

"She's right there, Daddy," Bobby says, pointing at me. I know it's not dark enough here to cloak me. I start to say, "No, that's okay," but my words grind to a halt.

Daniel is moving toward me, his hand outstretched.

I take his hand and move into the circle of his arms. The warmth of his touch makes me sigh; it is a sound I try to take back. In this darkness, it is too loud, too breathy.

We move together awkwardly; I wonder if it has been as long for him as it has for me. "I was never much of a dancer," I say by way of explanation. This is an understatement. Thom flat out refused to dance.

I can feel Daniel's gaze on me. "I can't see your feet, but I'll wager I'm steppin' on 'em," he says with a nervous laugh.

I feel young in his arms, and safe. We find a rhythm easily, and move together as if we've danced for years.

Overhead and to our right, a star tumbles through the sky in a streak of white. "Make a wish," he whispers.

My answer is **you,** but that's ridiculous. I don't think I could stand it if he laughed at me now, so I say, "I want to start over."

The music ends and Daniel releases me. It's all I can do not to reach for him. I know I will think about this moment, his touch, all night.

Behind us, Bobby flicks off the radio, plunges us all into the real world again. Now there is only the roar of the surf and the crackling of the fire. "I know my wish, Dad. What's yours?"

It's a long time before Daniel answers. When he does, he's looking at me. "Starting over would be nice."

I stare at Daniel, unable to look away, unable to stop thinking **what if?**

What if I could fall in love again and start my life over? What if I could belong here?

"Well, let's get going," he says at last. "We've lost our light."

At that, I think: Have we? Have we lost our light, or have we perhaps just glimpsed it for the first time? All I know is that, when I climb into the truck with this man and his son, I'm smiling.

Suddenly, I know what I have been waiting for all these years, why I've been collecting brochures and books and snapping pictures of other places.

I've been wanting to start over, dreaming of it.

And now, finally, I know where I want to be when I begin this new part of my life.

All that night, as I lie in my bed, I think of Daniel. Over and over in my mind, I replay our dancing. The way he looked at me, held me, whispered, "Make a wish." As the night rolls toward dawn, it takes on the shiny patina of myth.

I am just waking up when I hear a noise.

Footsteps on the stairs.

Daniel. I can tell by the sound.

I throw my covers back and get out of bed. A quick run into my bathroom, and I'm dressed. Then, carefully, I peer out my door.

A light is on in the lobby.

I walk quietly down the carpeted hallway. In the lobby, I find no one. It takes me a second to notice that the door is open.

In the purple mist of early morning, I see him standing in the front yard. This time, I don't even think about hanging back. I am starting over now; this is my new beginning.

I am almost beside him when I see Bobby out on the end of the dock. He is talking to the air. Even from this distance, I can see that he is crying and yelling.

Daniel makes a sound. In this foggy morning the sound is distorted, drawn out until it sounds like a sob.

I lay my hand on his arm. "I'm here," I say.

He shivers at my touch, but doesn't

turn to look at me. "God . . . how long will this go on?"

The truth is **forever** and **not long**. "He'll talk to her until he doesn't need to anymore."

We stand there, side by side. Out on the dock, Bobby is yelling for his mommy.

"He'll be okay," I say quietly. "He has a father who loves him. That would have made a difference to me. When my mom died, I mean. All I had was my sister."

Suddenly I'm thinking about Mom's funeral and how I'd fallen apart completely. Stacey was the glue that put me back together, held me together. She was my strength during Mom's long illness.

Stacey.

For the first time, I don't wince at the thought of her. The memory doesn't hurt: rather, it takes on the ache of longing. I have missed my sister; this is one of the many truths from which I've been running.

Bobby hurtles toward us.

Daniel immediately kneels. "I'm here, boyo."

Bobby skids to a stop. His cheeks are wet with tears, his eyes are bloodshot. "She didn't come. I yelled and yelled."

"Oh, Bobby," Daniel says, wiping his son's tears. I can see him struggling for the right words of comfort. We both know that Bobby needs to let go of his imaginary mother, but the letting go will hurt.

Daniel pulls Bobby into his arms and holds him tightly, whispering words in a lilting, song-like language I don't understand.

Bobby looks at him. "But I'm scared."

"Of what?"

"Forgetting her," Bobby says in a quiet, miserable way.

Daniel closes his eyes for a moment, and in this reaction I see how hurt he is by his son's revelation. When he opens his eyes, I can see the sheen of tears. "I should have done this a long time ago," he says.

"What?"

Daniel scoops Bobby into his arms and carries him into the house. "Wait here," he says, depositing his son on the sofa. He runs up the stairs.

Bobby looks so small, sitting there on the sofa, with his glistening cheeks and missing front tooth. "Did I do something wrong?" he asks me.

I sit down on the hearth across from him. I don't sit beside him because I want him to hear me. To listen. "Tell me about her."

"Mommy?" His voice breaks, but I can see how a smile wants to start. I wonder how long he has waited for someone to ask.

"She liked pink. And she talked really fast."

I smile at that. It reminds me of my own mom, who snorted when she laughed. Once, when I was little, she laughed so hard milk came out of her nose. It is a memory I thought I'd lost until just now. "My mom used to kiss my forehead to see if I had a fever. I loved that."

"My mommy used to wear butterflies in her hair when she got dressed up."

I lean forward. "You won't forget her, Bobby. I promise."

"You'll leave me, too, won't you? Just like her."

The question—and the sad resignation in his voice—is hard to hear. I know I shouldn't promise him anything—my life is in upheaval right now and the things I want may well exceed my grasp, but I can't just sit here and say nothing. "I have another life in California."

"You'll say good-bye, right? You won't just disappear."

My life might be mixed up, but this vow is easy to make. I'd never leave without saying good-bye. "I promise."

Daniel comes down the stairs, carrying a big brown photo album and a shoebox.

I stand, feeling shaky on my feet. This is a private moment. I don't belong here. "I should go. I've . . ."

"Don't go," Bobby says. "Tell her, Daddy. Tell Joy to stay."

"Please, Joy," he says, pulling Bobby close against him. "Don't go."

It is the way he says **please** that traps me; that, and the knowledge that Bobby is fragile now. I cross around the makeshift coffee table and sit down next to Daniel.

"Make room for her, Dad."

Daniels scoots toward his son.

"I have plenty of room," I say.

Bobby looks up at his dad. "Joy says I'll always remember things about Mommy. Like the butterfly clips she wore. And the way she gave me fish kisses at naptime."

"Fish kisses," Daniel says, his voice gruff. I know he's remembering her now, too.

"She always got the words wrong in the Winnie-the-Pooh song." Bobby's voice is stronger now, less uncertain.

"Her nighttime prayers went on forever," Daniel says, smiling now. "She blessed everyone she'd ever met." He looks down at Bobby. "And she loved you, boyo."

"You, too."

"Aye."

Daniel opens the photo album on his lap. There, in black and white is a series of pictures: a boy playing kick-the-can on dirty streets, and riding his rusty bike, and standing by a stone stacked fence, with a kite. The boy has jet black hair that needs a cut. **Daniel**.

There's another shot of a dirty street and a pub called the Pig-and-Whistle.

"That's Nana and Papa," Bobby says, pointing to the couple standing at the pub's wooden door. "They live in Boston now."

"Still spend their time hanging around the pubs," Daniel says, laughing as he turns the page.

Maggie.

Her face looks up at us, wreathed in bridal lace. She looks young and bright and gloriously happy. Her smile could light up Staples Center.

I can't help thinking of my own wedding album, tucked deep in an upstairs bookcase, gathering the dust of lost years.

I wonder if I'd even recognize my younger self, or would I look through the images of my own life like an archeologist, studying artifacts of an extinct race?

And what of Stacey? Can I really stay away from her wedding, her big moment? We have always been the witnesses of each other's lives. Isn't that what family is? Even broken and betrayed and bleeding, we are connected.

I push the thoughts aside and focus on the photographs in Daniel's album.

The next few pages contain dozens of wedding shots. Daniel goes through them without comment; I hear his relieved sigh when he comes to the end of them.

"There's me," Bobby says, pointing at the first photo of a baby so tiny his face looks like a pink quarter.

"Aye. That's the day we brought you home from the hospital."

"But Mommy's crying."

"That's because she loved you so much."

From there on, as Daniel turns the

pages, he talks, telling the story of their family in that musical brogue of his, and with every passing moment, every sylla-ble that sounds like a song lyric, I can see them moving closer together, this boy with a broken heart and the man who loves him.

"That's your first friend, your cousin Sean . . . your first birthday party . . . the day you said 'Mama.'"

In time, I begin to notice that there are fewer pictures of him and none of him and Maggie. The whole album is Bobby.

I know how a thing like this happens. Not all at once, but day by day. You stop wanting to record every minute of an un-happy life. In Bakersfield, I have a drawer of similar albums, where the oldest ver-sions are of Thom and me, and the new-est ones are mostly scenery.

By the time Daniel reaches the last page, Bobby is asleep, tucked in close to his father. Daniel says softly, "Joy?"

At my name, whispered as it is in the quiet between us, he sighs and smiles.

"I'm here," I say, waiting for more.

When he says nothing, I decide to be bold. I lean toward him, say, "Maybe you and I . . ." I don't know how to finish, how to ask for what I want, but it doesn't matter. I've gone too far, revealed too much. Daniel shakes his head and pulls away from me.

"I'm losing my mind," he says without looking at me. Then, he gets up from the sofa and carries Bobby to the stairs.

What was I thinking to say "you and I" with the photographs of his lost wife between us?

As always, I am a master at timing.

Once again, I am alone.

SEVEN

I try to fall back asleep, but after the predawn show, it's impossible. Somewhere around seven o'clock, I give up and take a shower. I am in the kitchen, looking for coffee when I hear footsteps on the stairs, then in the hallway. I turn just in time to see Daniel coming in to the room. He looks haggard, worn down. The lines around his eyes are so deep and dark they appear to be drawn in charcoal.

He sees me and the coffeemaker, in that order, and he smiles. "Ah, coffee."

"I guess we have an addiction in common. That, and wanting to start over." The minute the words are out of my mouth, I want to call them back. Even worse than the words is my voice; it's all breathy, Marilyn-Monroe-Mr.-Presidenty.

He stares at me a moment longer, then leaves the room.

I stand there, feeling like a fool. Everything I say to Daniel is wrong.

It's hardly surprising. I haven't exactly had a lot of experience. There was Jed Breen in high school and Jerry Wist the summer after graduation, but that's all. I met Thom at a party in my sophomore year at Davis, and Lord knows I haven't dated since our divorce.

Sipping my coffee, I head out of the kitchen.

Bobby runs up to me, as if he's been waiting. "Teach me more reading."

"Sure."

He leads me to the sofa. For hours, we sit there, sounding out sentences. I praise and encourage him, but all the while I'm also listening for footsteps on the deck. I keep remembering my dance with

Daniel. **Make a wish. Starting over would be . . .**

"Joy," Bobby says. "JOY."

I blink, come into the now. "Sorry, Bobby." I'm like a teenager, mooning over a boy. The thought makes me smile. Who would have thought?

"What's this word?"

I turn my attention back to the book that's open in my lap. It's the Disney version of **Pinocchio,** and Bobby has an endless appetite for the story of the wooden boy who wants to be real. This is the second read of the day. "R . . . E . . . A . . . L. Real."

He looks up at me. "I wish the Blue Fairy would make Freddy real."

If the Blue Fairy existed, Freddy would be knee-deep in clover. Heaven knows the stuffed lamb with the straggly fur and loose button eye has been loved.

Behind us, the door bangs open.

Bobby slams the book shut. He wants to surprise Daniel with his reading.

Daniel walks in to the lobby, his flannel shirt and down vest peppered with sawdust and rain. His face is gray with wet dirt. When he smiles, his teeth are brilliant white. "Hey, there." He takes off his jacket, lays it on the chair back, then turns on the television. "It's no use workin' any more. A storm is coming."

"A storm?" Bobby sounds scared.

"Don't worry, boyo. I'm here to protect you."

Bobby tucks in closer to me, whining. "I **hate** storms."

For the first time, I notice how dark it is in the lobby. Outside, charcoal clouds obliterate the sky overhead. Shadows crawl across the lake and grass.

"Turn on the news, will you, Bobby?" Daniel says, bending over to unbutton his work boots. "I'll be back down in a sec." With that, he goes upstairs.

Bobby reaches for the remote and hits the power button. There is a thump of sound, then a picture.

"I hate the news," he mutters, eying the darkening day outside.

On screen, a pretty blond woman is talking about a three-alarm fire in downtown Seattle. After that, she relays the rest of the local news: a few burglaries, a car stolen in Hoquiam, and a goat mascot stolen from a nearby high school.

They show a series of local homes, decked out for the holidays, even giving out the addresses so people can drive by to see the displays.

We have different drive-bys in Southern California.

Outside, thunder rolls. Lightning flares.

Bobby screams. I reach for him, saying, "Don't worry, I'm . . ."

Then I hear: **plane crash**. I want to say, "Turn off the set! Change the channel!" But I can't speak. Instead, I get to my feet, take a step forward.

". . . nearly eighty miles north of here. As reported earlier, the eleven named

passengers on the charter flight were rescued by firefighters on Friday evening
and taken to local hospitals."

The picture from my driver's license
fills the screen.

"Joy Faith Candellaro," the anchor-
woman says pleasantly, as if she's relaying
a tuna casserole recipe and not news of a
missing person, "from Bakersfield, California. When the director of the charter
flight, Riegert Milosovich, regained consciousness following surgery, he told authorities that this woman had purchased
a ticket at the last moment and had been
onboard the plane when . . ."

"Is the thunder done?" Bobby asks
nervously.

"Just a minute, Bobby." White noise
roars in my head, blocking out the
broadcast. I'm trying to hear the words
when the picture onscreen changes and
I gasp.

It's Stacey; she is standing in front of
her three-car garage, crying. In a pale yel-

low sweatshirt and matching pants (which I gave her for her birthday last year), she looks washed out and colorless. "We're praying she comes back to us." She glances at Thom, who looks surprisingly shaken. Is he **crying**? "It's the season of miracles, right?" Stacey says to the reporter.

"That lady looks like you," Bobby says, pointing at my sister.

"Really?" I answer dully. I've heard it all my life. Irish twins. Two sisters, only a year apart in age, who were always there for each other.

"She sure is sad."

Who would have thought she'd miss me so much?

But that is a lie. I see the truth I've hidden from myself all these days and nights. I **knew** Stacey would miss me, weep for me. I wanted that, wanted her to regret what she'd done to me.

I wanted to break her heart, like she'd broken mine.

But it is one thing to want Stacey to feel bad for me, it's something else to let her believe I'm dead.

My vacation is over.

"What's the matter, Joy?"

Thunder rolls outside, shaking the lodge. The windows rattle at the storm.

Bobby screams: "Daddy!" and leaps off the couch.

Daniel is down the stairs in an instant, scooping Bobby into his arms. "It's just a storm, boyo," he says soothingly, "nothing to be afraid of."

"He's right, Bobby. There's nothing to be scared of, " I say dully, but even as I say the words, I know they are a lie. There **is** something to be scared of now for Bobby and for me. I have to go home.

Lightning flashes into the room, turning everything blue-white for an instant. I look at Daniel, who is holding his son tightly, and Bobby, whose small, pale face is ruined by tears.

"It's like when Mommy . . ."

"Shhh," Daniel says. "Shhh." He

turns, carrying Bobby upstairs. I can hear their voices. Soft. Uncertain.

Daniel is singing to Bobby; the hushed notes of the song underscore the sounds of crying. It's a song I don't recognize, and I don't understand the words, but it moves me nonetheless, makes me think about the times in my life—long ago now—when I felt safe and loved.

I feel my way to the registration desk and find the phone. It's time to call Stacey. Lightning is a strobe light that turns off and on, blasting me in and out of darkness.

I pick up the phone and call the operator. There are two rings, then, the electricity snaps off, the phone goes dead, and everything goes dark.

In my dreams, the world is full of strange noises and unfamiliar smells.

Light. It is buzzing all around me like bees around the comb. There is a **thunk-**

whoosh sound that repeats itself, over and over.

It's the surf at the beach they called Kalaloch; I hear the waves whispering to me, calling me to come forward, feel their coolness. I feel as if I'm being held under the water. I can't breathe. Panicked, I try to fight my way to the surface, but it's useless.

"Joy, wake up."

"Wake up. Pleease."

It's my sister's voice.

I'm out of the ocean now. For a blissful moment I'm ten years old again, and we're at a KOA campground in Needles, California. Stacey wants to break the rules, go swimming at night in the pool by the registration building. She is tugging on my sleeve.

Then I'm back on Madrona Lane, close enough to touch my pregnant sister and yet unable to reach out. The wedding invitation is on the asphalt between us. **Thomas James Candellaro and**

Stacey Elizabeth McAvoy request your presence . . .

"Wake up, Joy."

Someone touches my arm, pushes me gently.

I open my eyes, disoriented at first by the shadowy darkness around me. I expected to be at home, staring up at my own ceiling, listening to the sound of old Mr. Lundgren's lawn mower.

Bobby is beside my bed, looking down at me.

I push to my elbows, shove the tangled red hair from my eyes. "Bobby," I say, trying to get past my dream. Everything is still watery, confusing. I can't remember a sleep so deep.

"You wouldn't wake up," he says, his eyes full of worry.

"I was up late last night," I say, as if he can understand the kind of sleepless night that comes with regret.

"I dreamed you went away."

I close my eyes and sigh. How could I

have blithely befriended him and not seen how all this would end?

Fantasies.

I've wrapped myself in them, let pretty images from an impossible future be my safety net, my safe place to land. I've thought of my time here as an adventure. In truth, it was an escape. All along, the clock on my discovery has been ticking. I simply didn't hear it before.

"Are you leaving?"

I want to lie to him; more than that, I want my lie to be the truth.

But I don't belong in this wild place, no matter how much I want to. This is the truth I stumbled upon in the dark last night as I tried to sleep. Daniel has never even hinted that he feels something for me. All my "what ifs" were really "if onlys."

I have been like Bobby, a child chasing a ghost on a dock at dawn.

I touch Bobby's plump cheek. In no time at all, his skin will roughen and grow hair. He will be a young man, and I will be a memory of his childhood.

"I want you to stay," he says, his voice unsteady.

Later, I will let myself feel the ache of those words. Now, I do not dare. "You have a daddy who loves you. And I have . . . a sister who tried to ask for my forgiveness. I need to go back to her. That's what I've learned here—from you and your daddy."

"But if you leave, I'll miss you. Don't you care about that?"

I can hardly answer; the tears are so full in my throat. "I do care about that, Bobby."

He stares at me through damp, accusing eyes. "Will you stay for Christmas morning? We can open presents."

"I don't . . ."

"Pleease?"

How can I say no? Especially when I want it so badly? I'll call Stacey and let her know I'm okay. Then I'll end my adventure with Christmas morning in this place I've come to love. And then I sigh. "I'll stay for Christmas morning, but then I'll need to leave. Okay?"

"You promise you'll stay?"

"I promise."

He barely smiles.

We both know it's not good enough. It's not what either of us wants.

But it's all there is.

By the time I've taken my shower and had breakfast, it's nearly ten.

I leave my room—or mean to—but as I step across the threshold, I stumble and fall into the doorway. Righting myself, I look back at this small, shabby space. Room 1A in a run-down fishing lodge with a ridiculous name.

And I know how much I will miss it. Whenever I close my eyes, I see this room as it could be, as I've imagined it: the log walls scrubbed to perfection and oiled to a glossy shine; the green carpet gone, in its stead the wide-plank pine boards that lie beneath; a pretty white wrought-iron bed, covered with hand-made quilts and lavender-blue throw pillows—exactly the hue of the night sky just before the sun sets. Fresh flowers on the antique dresser. A bathroom redone in white tile and brass, with a claw-foot tub.

I close the door on the image and walk away. My footsteps are soundless on the olive green carpeting. In the kitchen, I find a tray filled with fruit and cheese slices on the counter, and an otherwise empty room. I don't need to go upstairs (not that I would) to know that Daniel and Bobby are gone. I've come to know the moods of this place, the feel of it when people are here, and when they're gone. There are no creaking floorboards overhead, no fluttering fall of dust from the ceiling as Bobby rides his skateboard in the halls upstairs. The Christmas tree lights are off and the registration desk is dark.

I go to the window, just to be sure.

Outside, the storm has paused; clouds squat above the trees; the wind blows leaves across the deck and pushes at the trees as if they are bendable toys. But it isn't raining.

The truck is gone.

I look around for a note, knowing I won't find one. I'm a guest. Why would they let me know where they've gone or when they'll be back? Still, I can't help feeling disappointed.

I stand there a long time. Finally, I go to the phone and pick it up. The receiver feels cold against my ear.

There is still no dial tone.

I feel a rush of relief, but it doesn't last long. As much as I'd like to, I can't stay here, alone, hiding out from the world, my world. My Christmas gift to Stacey will be a phone call. Just that, a call, but it will be a start. Who knows where we'll go from there?

So I go to my room and get my borrowed blue sweater from the closet, then I find an umbrella behind the registration desk—just in case—and I'm off.

Wind blows down the road and whistles through the trees. The forest is darker than usual, as is the sky.

I follow the winding black ribbon of asphalt that parallels the lake. Leaves and debris skid down the pavement, blow past me. Brown water gurgles in the ditches.

I angle against the wind, trudging forward, sloshing through dips and puddles from last night's storm. Ahead of me, the road shimmers with water.

At first, I walk at a pretty good pace. I'm in decent shape, after all, I do aerobics on a quasi-regular basis, and I've lost weight in the past week. I feel thinner, anyway. I haven't actually stepped on a scale.

Every bend in the road promises to be "The One." I keep expecting to see the town spread out before me, a tiny tiara of holiday lights tucked in to all this stormy darkness.

But every corner leads to another straightaway. This old highway goes on and on.

I am losing steam, which seems odd because my breath is a series of white clouds, shooting out in front of me. The steps get harder. It's cold. Wind scratches my face, tugs at my hair.

I can't believe I walked this far after the crash. Then, it had felt like nothing, this trek through the ancient woods. In truth, it's miles.

How could I have done it?

On and on I go, until I truly begin to consider turning back.

I am all alone out here. In the time I've been walking, no cars have passed me, no headlights have cut down the pavement to show me the way back, even for a fifty-five mile-per-hour moment. Black clouds hang ominously low in the sky, make this afternoon almost dark.

Up ahead, there is another bend in the road.

"That's it," I say aloud. I will turn around if town isn't around the corner.

Then, in the distance, I hear cars.

Thank God.

The walking is easier again, with the end in sight. I pick up my pace a little, until I'm breathless when I finally come to town.

I leave the two-lane highway and turn onto a pretty little tree-lined street called Azalea. I have gone fifty feet or so when it hits me.

The lights are out here, too.

The town is dark; buildings seem smaller without light, bunched together, as if they're huddling to keep warm.

In the gray patch of the park, I see an old-fashioned phone booth on the corner. It's something I haven't seen in a while. In my part of California, the world has gone cellular, moved on from these glass-walled booths.

I duck inside, close the door behind me. No light comes on at the motion. I know before I pick up the phone what I will find.

It's dead. There is no phonebook hanging from a rusty chain.

When I step outside the booth, thunder grumbles across the slate-colored sky. Lightning flashes strobe-like, electrifying the sleepy town for a second. Then it starts to rain.

Hard.

I grab my umbrella and pop it open. Rain is thunderous on the plastic dome over my head. I run across the park.

In town, the eaves protect me. I walk close to the buildings, seeing even in the shadows how well tended everything is. Holiday decorations fill every window. At a diner called the "Dew Drop In," I see a "CLOSED: No Juice" sign that makes me smile in spite of how cold and miserable I am.

At the end of the street, I come to a four-way stop and turn right because the eaves protect me.

Two blocks later I see the impossible:

a gas station with its lights on. They must have a generator.

I rush across the wet, slick street and go to the door. Inside, it's a mini-mart with rows and rows of brightly colored merchandise. The lights are so bright I have to squint.

Behind the counter, a man is reading something from a manila folder and making notes on a clipboard of some kind. A slim gray cell phone sits on the counter by his right hand.

"Thank God," I say, tossing my dripping umbrella to the linoleum floor. "This storm is crazy, isn't it?"

He looks up at me, obviously surprised that anyone is out in this weather. He is thin-faced, with elegantly cut white hair and blue eyes that seem surprisingly sharp for a man of his age. "There's no way to know how long it'll last."

It's the same thing the weathermen always say. I smile at him. "I need to use your phone."

He stares at me oddly and taps at the

hearing aid in his left ear. "Broken bones?"

"Not bones. **Phone**. I need to make a call. Collect."

"Can you hear me?" he says, leaning closer. "It's broken."

"I hear **you**," I say, trying to keep the impatience out of my voice. I'm tired, soaking wet, and freezing cold. It would be easy to snap, so I take a deep breath and try to smile. "I know the electricity is out." I tap his cell phone. "May I use it? **Please?** I need to talk to my sister."

At that, he smiles, showing me a hint of flawless white dentures, and tugs at his ear, which—surprisingly—sports an earring that looks like a tiny diamond. "Talking is good."

The poor man is deaf as a post. If I weren't freezing and desperate, I'd be polite. As it is, I say, "Yes, it is. Look. I'm using your phone. I hope you don't mind."

"The mind is a delicate thing."

"That's helpful. Thank you." I reach for his phone. Every second, as I flip it open and punch in the numbers, I expect him to stop me, but he doesn't. He simply goes back to his reading.

The phone rings.

And rings.

At each bleating ring, I tense up a little more. Finally, the machine clicks on. It's Stacey's voice. **Happy holidays. Stacey and Thom aren't in right now, but if you'll leave a message, we'll call you back. Thanks!**

I'm momentarily nonplussed by the casual linking of their names. Staceyandthom. Thomandstacey. Now they're one word, just like we used to be.

"Uh . . . Hi, Stace. It's Joy. I'm fine. You don't need to worry. I'll call you on Christmas Day." It seems like I should have more to say, but nothing comes to me. "Bye."

I hang up and hand the phone back to the attendant. "Thanks."

He peers at me. "You can keep talking to her."

"No, thanks. I'm done."

Smiling, I grab my umbrella and leave the warm light of the gas station.

It's not until I'm back in the park, trudging through the now blinding rain that I think: I should have asked him for a ride home. This is Small Town, U.S.A. People do favors for each other here. I turn back, walk down the street. Thunder roars again; the rain hammers me.

In the violence of the storm, I'm confused, though, disoriented; I can't find the gas station again.

I have always had a crappy sense of direction.

With a sigh, I head for the park, and then find my way onto the old highway. My first thought is: this is the way home.

Then I remember.

My home sits on a pretty little street in a not-so-pretty section of Bakersfield, the same city where my pregnant sister and ex-husband now live together.

Staceyandthom.

What will I say to them?

EIGHT

*J*ust when I think the weather can't get any worse, it starts to snow.

In an instant, this stormy landscape changes into a place of magical, impossible light. The clouds lift, a bright moon peers out from above and casts the road in silvery light. The driving rain transforms itself into a shower of tiny cotton balls, drifting lazily downward.

Everything stills; the world holds its breath. The gurgling water in the ditch turns into a child's laugh. I can smell the pine trees again, and the rich scent of wet earth.

Unfortunately, the sudden beauty has a wicked bite.

It's **cold**.

Inside my suddenly inadequate sweater, I shiver and try to keep warm. My breath clouds everything, makes me feel as if I'm walking through a deep fog.

Once I start shivering, I can't stop. I must look like an escaped mental patient, running from the electrical shock room, dancing along the crumbling edge of the road. I am so tired; all I want to do is stop, but I know that if I do, I'll fall, and maybe I won't get up. My eyelids are heavy, my fingers and toes sting with cold. My cheeks are so icy they feel hot; every snowflake burns my skin. Only a woman raised in California would have gone for a walk on a day like this.

"Don't th-think like that," I say aloud, trying to sound stern and failing miserably. My teeth are chattering like an Evinrude. I need to focus on good thoughts.

Like the lodge, dressed in its holiday finery, with Bobby and Daniel on the deck, waiting for me.

Are they home? I wonder. Have they noticed that I am gone? Are they worried?

How long has it been since someone waited at home for me, worried about me?

Stacey.

Even with all that has happened; all she has done, the truth is there, buried beneath the resentment: I miss her.

She is the one I want to tell about my time in the rainforest, and the man and boy about whom I've come to care.

I guess a plane crash and being lost in a snowstorm will show you things.

I am caught so deeply in my own thoughts that it takes me a moment to hear the noise behind me.

It is an engine. Seconds later, I see the twin beams of headlights come up behind me. In their glow, I see the snow falling all around me.

I stop, turn.

It is Daniel's red pickup, chugging down the road. They are like something out of a dream, a blur of red in a snowy white world. I'm not entirely sure it's real. Perhaps I've imagined my saviors.

The truck pulls up beside me and stops. The blue passenger door creaks, then bangs open.

Bobby is scooted all the way to the edge of the bench seat. His small face is scrunched with worry and too colorful somehow in this hazy world and half-light. "Joy?"

I try to answer, to smile even, as if this is nothing, but all I hear is the sound of my own teeth chattering. Suddenly I'm crying like a baby. That's when I realize how scared I was that I would be simply lost out here, all alone again. No wonder I thought of Stacey.

"Help her, Dad!" Bobby cries out. "She's freezing!"

Daniel whips open his door and jumps out.

"I'm . . . fine," I say, sounding like a jackhammer on concrete. I grab the top of the truck door—the metal is so cold it burns me—and climb into the seat. I don't want him to know how cold I am, how foolish I was. I could have died out here. "Th-thanks."

Standing by the side of the truck, Daniel looks worriedly through the cab at me. He's probably never seen a woman with blue cheeks before. There's a strange look in his eyes, one I can't read. It's more than just worry, though. I think he's angry with me for being so stupid, for scaring his son. He climbs back into the driver's seat and slams the door shut. "A person could die in this weather," he says softly.

"I'm fine. Really. I was just . . . trying to find a phone to call my sister. I'm sorry to have worried you."

"Daddy has a cell phone," Bobby says accusingly. I can tell how upset he is. He thought I'd simply left without a word. Disappeared like his mother.

I have no answer to that. My actions were stupid. Plain stupid.

"We've been driving around for **hours** looking for you," Bobby says. I can hear the panic in his voice. "I **told** him you were in trouble."

"I promised you Christmas morning," I say quietly. "Remember? I just needed to make a phone call. Honest."

"Okay," he says, still looking un-convinced.

I dare to glance at Daniel. "Bobby in-vited me to spend Christmas morning with you."

"I told Daddy that you were staying for Christmas and then leaving."

Daniel still doesn't look at me. Driving in snow takes all his concentra-tion. Or, perhaps, he wants Christmas morning with only his son.

Before, in my life, I would have been silent now, waited for him to invite me, to want me, but somewhere along the way of this adventure, I've grown bold. Life can be short. Planes can simply fall out of the sky; sisters can lose the chance they need. "What do you think of that, Daniel?"

In the silence that follows my question, the windshield wipers seemed almost obscenely loud. He can hurt me now, ruin me with a look or a smile, but I take this risk. It's what I want: Christmas with Bobby and Daniel. Then I'll go back to Bakersfield. Every heartbeat that he doesn't answer wounds me. It's crazy, I know, and naïve, but I can't help it.

Bobby must sense the tension and feel for me. "Daddy?" he says when the quiet has gone on for almost a mile. "You want Joy to stay for Christmas, don't you?"

I draw in a sharp breath, but Daniel doesn't turn to me. Quietly, he says, "Of course I do."

Of course.

As if my question were unnecessary. The tension seeps out of me, leaving me strangely limp. I lean back into the seat.

Daniel turns on the radio. "Jingle Bell Rock" blares from the speakers, making me smile. My mom loved this song.

"What does your family do for Christmas morning?" Bobby asks me.

"We go to church."

"That's what me and Mommy used to do."

"I light a candle for my mom," I add. "So she knows how much I still love her."

"Would you light one for my mommy?"

"If you'll come to church with me, I will."

A long moment passes, punctuated by the thunk of the wipers. Then, quietly, he says, "Okay."

I look down at him, feeling tears sting my eyes. The courage of this boy slays me. "We can pray for her together."

"Okay what?" Daniel says, frowning as if he's missed something. He turns down the radio.

"Joy's gonna help me light a candle for Mommy on Christmas morning."

"In church?"

Bobby nods.

I can she how moved Daniel is by those few words. He doesn't look at his son or me; I suspect if he did that his eyes would be moist. "I can see how Joy got her name."

Daniel's voice is so soft and warm. It wraps around me like a blanket. Smiling, I rest my head against the cool window and close my eyes. All at once I'm exhausted.

Daniel pulls into the lodge parking lot and shuts off the ignition. He immediately turns to Bobby. "Come here."

Bobby launches himself at his dad.

"I'm so proud of you, boyo."

"But I don't want Joy to leave."

"I know."

I sit up slowly. An ache blossoms in my chest at the sight of them. If ever I am inclined in the future to disbelieve in love, I will remember this moment.

Daniel tightens his hold on his son. "You're my whole world, Bobby. You know that, don't you? We're a team now. You and me."

"What if Joy comes back later? Can she be part of us?"

Daniel smiles. He looks younger suddenly, unburdened.

I catch my breath. It would be so easy to lose myself in Daniel's eyes, and find myself in his world.

"Maybe, boyo," Daniel says, looking at me over Bobby's head. "A thing like that comes down to . . . I don't know."

"Fate."

We whisper the word at the same time, Daniel and I. It seems as soft as a love song in the cab, and as sturdy as one of these old trees.

But Bobby wants something more concrete. "If she comes back, can she stay with us?"

Daniel is frowning suddenly. I wonder if, like me, he's come undone by the single word that somehow joins us, gives us a glimpse of **maybe**. "Sure."

"You promise?" Bobby says.

"I promise," Daniel answers, still gazing at me. I feel something waken in me, a longing that makes my heart speed up. "All she has to do is say, 'Open the damn door, Daniel. It's cold out here,' and I'll let her in.' "

Bobby laughs. It is the purest, clearest sound I've ever heard. "She doesn't **swear,** Dad."

For the first time, Daniel and I laugh together.

The best pieces of chocolate in the box are always the last ones. So it is with this second-to-last night I have at the Comfort Fishing Lodge. By the time we get home, the electricity is back on. In no time, the Christmas tree and mantel are pockets of glowing colored lights and there's a roaring fire in the fireplace.

Bobby and Daniel go to the kitchen for dinner; I go to my room and take a shower. I'm cold to the bone; food is the last thing on my mind.

Rather, I think about tomorrow.

Christmas Eve.

It will be my last night here.

Already I know that my vacation is

over. When Stacey gets home—probably from Thom's office party—she'll listen to my message and immediately start looking for me. I'll be "big news." The authorities will clamor for answers to questions I don't want voiced, let alone answered. I don't believe any of them will understand why I chose to walk away from the crash.

The few who **will** understand will be those who have been where I was in early December. People who have lost themselves in the dark woods of ordinary life, who have been betrayed by loved ones and forgotten how to be led by dreams.

And Daniel.

For no reason I can articulate, I am sure he will understand my bizarre choice. He is a man who knows about drifting, about betrayal and loss. I'm certain of it. It's why he bought this place, those years ago when his family lived amid the red brick of Boston. Sometimes a change of scenery can be the answer. Or an answer, anyway.

Stacey, too, will understand, and she will forgive me. The question is: can I forgive her? Even with all that I have learned, I don't know the answer to that, and truthfully, I don't want to think about it. I haven't much time here at the Comfort Lodge. I need to soak up every second and fashion the time into memories. I will need them when I'm home again.

It is the need for **more** that sends me in search of them again. I go out to the lobby, where Bobby and Daniel are watching **Miracle on 34th Street**.

"Oh, good," Bobby says at my arrival. "You didn't miss anything."

He doesn't yet know how many times we watch Christmas movies in our lives. I take a seat in the red leather chair by the fireplace.

Together—like a family—we watch the movie.

As I watch the scenes unfurl, I can't help thinking of other Christmases, long ago.

"My mommy loved this part," Bobby says softly.

Onscreen, a young Natalie Wood is running through her new house, finding the cane that proves a miracle.

"Mine, too," I say as the screen goes black and the credits roll.

Bobby's smile dips for a second, then returns. "You wanna play Chutes and Ladders?"

"Of course," I answer.

Daniel laughs. "It's better than watching the Grinch again."

Bobby laughs at that, and the sound of their braided laughter—Daniel's throaty and full, his son's high and childish—finds a soft spot in me.

Bobby runs upstairs and is back in no time. Within minutes, the game is set up on the card table.

Daniel sits on the hearth facing the game. The fire backlights him. It is impossible not to notice how handsome he is. "Well, boyo," he says, rubbing his hands together, "you ready for a whoopin'?"

Bobby giggles and sets out our pieces. I sit in the empty chair to Daniel's left. Bobby sits across from me. "I get to move for everyone," he says, trying to stack the cards on the place where they go.

"Aye," Daniel says. "You always do. Just like you open everyone's presents."

For the next hour, Bobby leads us around the board. He picks all the cards and moves all the pieces and laughs whenever he pulls ahead. Daniel and I can hardly get a word in edgewise, but, in truth, we're not trying very hard. I can tell that Daniel is captivated by his son's smile, and I am mesmerized by the pair of them.

Unlike me, Bobby will never know the nagging ache of an absent father; he will have the loss of his mother inside him, like a thin shadow on a bright day, standing close, but he won't have that dragging sense that he was unloved, somehow, unworthy. For the whole of his life, he will go to sleep at night knowing his father loves him.

"You sure are laughin' a lot tonight, boyo." Daniel's voice pulls me back into the moment.

"Joy keeps getting the **worst** cards," he answers with a giggle.

"It's hardly my fault." When I look up from the board, I catch Daniel's gaze and wonder if he sees who we could be together. I try to come up with a gem of a remark—one that will make him want me the way I'm beginning to want him—but nothing comes to me, and the moment moves on.

As the night darkens, and we go from Chutes and Ladders to Candy Land, I have to keep reminding myself that I'm a guest here. Otherwise, I'll reach for Daniel. I'll touch his arm and say something stupid like "Are you lonely, too?" or "Do you feel it, this spark?" It takes all my self-control to say nothing of importance. Each moment I'm silent, I know, is a moment lost, a second that brings me closer to good-bye.

This night—and everything it represents—is the dream I've held onto all my life. A family held together by love, a child who needs me. A man who knows how to love. I want so desperately to belong here, to be invited to stay. I could start over here, maybe get a job at the local high school and help Daniel refurbish this place. I'd be good at it; I know I would. If only he'd ask me. If only I had the courage to say it first.

"You have to go all the way back," Bobby giggles, looking at my card. "Look, Dad, Mommy has to go back."

Suddenly the crackling of the fire is loud in the room, as is Daniel's indrawn breath.

"I mean Joy," Bobby chirps happily, moving my man back.

Daniel looks at Bobby; his face is pale, his lips tight. I don't know him well enough to read his expression. Is it fear that Bobby has come to love me too much? Or regret that some things longed for can't be had? Or is it grief for the woman who should be at this game table on this night? I don't know. All I know is that I wish he'd looked at me, if even just for an instant, and smiled. Instead, I see how he avoids looking at me in this moment where I've been called Mommy for the first time in my life.

"It's your turn, Dad," Bobby says, reaching for another card.

And the game goes on. I try to forget that Bobby called me Mommy and that Daniel looked so hurt by it, but I can't. It makes me **want**—that single word and all that it implies.

Mommy.

I learn something about myself this cold winter's night. Something I should have known, perhaps; had I known it, I never would have walked away from the crash site.

You can run away from your life and

your past, but there's no way to distance
yourself from your own heart.

At eight o'clock, Daniel ends our perfect
evening.

"I know a boy who needs to get ready
for bed," he says, standing up.

"Aw, Dad," Bobby whines, making a
face. He is getting up from his chair
when he smiles. "But Joy and me hafta
wrap your present."

Daniel looks down at his son. "Now?"

"Tomorrow is Christmas Eve," I say to
Daniel. "All presents need to be under
the tree."

Daniel isn't fooled. "You just want to
stay up. Okay. I have a few presents of
my own to wrap, but I want you upstairs
by eight-thirty. Should I set the timer on
the oven to remind you?"

"No way."

"I'll make sure he's on time," I say.

Daniel stands there a moment longer,

looking at us. Bobby is right beside me now. He's so excited his little body seems to be vibrating.

"Okay then," Daniel finally says. "See you in half an hour."

When he is gone, Bobby runs to the sofa and pulls his copy of **Green Eggs and Ham** out from under the cushion. "I need to practice one more time, okay?"

"Sure."

We settle into the comfortable cushions together and open the book.

"I . . . am . . . Sam. Sam . . . I . . . am." Bobby has memorized this part of the book, so he runs through it quickly. By the time he gets to page sixteen, he has slowed down and begun to sound out the words. "**I** . . . w . . . ou . . . l . . . d **would** not like th . . . em **them** h . . . ere **here** or th . . . ere **there**."

I tighten my hold on him.

By the time he finishes the book, his smile is so big it's like a storm wave breaking over the beach. Uncontainable.

"This is the best present you could give your dad."

"Arnie Holtzner won't call me stupid now." He twists around to look up at me. "Thanks." He says it quietly, but it still hits me hard.

"You're welcome." I lean toward him and gently kiss his forehead. It should be a perfect moment, a memory to take away with me, but when I feel the velvet of his warm skin and breathe in the sweet citrus scent of his hair, all I can think about is how it will feel to say good-bye.

I ease back from him, trying to smile. "We've got a few more minutes before your dad is expecting you. Will you help me with something?"

"Sure."

"I need a piece of paper and some-thing to write with."

Bobby slides eel-like off the sofa and runs to the registration desk. He is back in mere moments, holding a yellow legal pad and a red crayon.

I can't help smiling. I haven't written

with a crayon in years. "Okay. Let's go to the card table."

We clear the game and take our seats, side by side, tucking in close. I hand Bobby the crayon and position the pad in front of him. "You're going to write a list out for me. It's your dad's Christmas present from me."

"I can't . . ."

"Yes, you can. It's good practice. I'll tell you the words and you sound them out and write them down. It'll make my present extra special."

He looks so scared I want to hug him. Instead, I don my best teacher's face and say, "The first word is **ideas**. I . . . d . . . e . . . a . . . s." I help him sound it out but let him spell it himself.

The crayon quivers in his hand. He holds it tightly, fisting it, and bends over the paper. "Go slow," he says, frowning in concentration.

It takes almost fifteen minutes of working together, but in the end, we have a list that looks like this:

Ibeas.
  chng nme/rmantic
  pant trm
    flwrs
     fix cbns
      websit
       no crpt flr

"Wow," Bobby says when we're done. "My mom wanted to do some of these things. You think he'll do it? I wish—"

"I know." I don't want him to say his hope out loud. Some things need to be simply planted in the soft dirt of possibility. "But you remember this, Bobby: What matters is you and your dad being together. You guys are a team now. A family."

Bobby looks up at me. "You'll come back someday, won't you, Joy?"

"Wild horses couldn't keep me away. Now, let's wrap this present up and put it under the tree."

I show Bobby how to roll the list into a cylinder and wrap it in the pretty red foil paper, then to coil ribbons on each end. When we're finished, the clock reads 8:25. "Time for you to go."

He grumbles in protest but heads dutifully for the stairs.

After he's gone, I sit on the hearth, listening to the last strains of the fading fire.

I have one more gift to place beneath the tree for Christmas morning—if I can find what I am looking for.

I go to my room and retrieve the still damp sweater I wore to town. Shrugging into it, I head outside.

The night is quiet and cold. A slushy layer of newly fallen snow covers the ground. Already it is beginning to melt. The green lawn shows through in big, irregular patches. Water drips from the eaves and branches, makes tiny dark holes in the melting snow.

I walk down the uneven path toward the lake.

As if on cue, the cloud overhead drifts on, revealing a nearly full moon. Shimmery blue light falls on me, on the lake and the clock, and the dark ground. It is almost eerie, this light, vaguely impossible. A shiver runs through me. Although it can't happen, I **know** it can't, I hear a woman's voice. It is quiet, barely above a whisper, but I hear it nonetheless, hear her say, "There."

I look down. There, lying all alone on top of a bed of shiny black stones, is a bright white arrowhead. Moonlight hits it and reflects it back at me, turning it for a second into a fallen star.

I spin around, but there is no woman around me.

Of course there isn't.

I bend down for the arrowhead. It fits perfectly in my palm, feels as smooth as silk and as cold as a snowflake. I tuck it into my pocket and walk back to the lodge, through a night that is both silvery light and jet black.

By the time I get to the door, I've told myself in no uncertain terms that nothing unusual happened by the lake.

I merely went in search of an arrowhead and found one.

But as I step onto the deck, hear it creak beneath my feet, I say softly, "Thanks, Maggie."

Then I go inside.

NINE

By morning, the snow is almost gone. I stand at my window, staring out at the green, sunlit backyard. I can see a corner of one of the cabins. The roof shingles are furred with thick moss. Come spring, I imagine that tiny flowers will sprout up from the mossy patches.

I should have added power-wash roofs to my list. And advertising in more in-flight magazines. I'll have to tell Daniel those things face-to-face.

Outside, on this Christmas Eve, the day is both sunlit and gray. A light rain is falling; the drops are so thin and tiny they're almost imaginary, like tears.

And suddenly I am thinking of Stacey.

I remember that last night in Bakersfield when she asked me to come to her wedding. And showed me her pregnant stomach.

I'm sorry, she'd said.

I remember her on television, crying for me, believing in the miracle of my return, hoping for it.

And Thom. The man I vowed to love forever, who now loves my sister.

The thought makes me sad, but doesn't ruin me anymore. I can actually think of them together without wincing.

If nothing else, this pause has given me that: a lens through which to view my previous life. It's not forgiveness. Not even near that yet, but it is . . . acceptance, and that's better than nothing.

I'm not sure how long I stand at my window, staring out, thinking about my life Before and what will happen tomorrow. Time is odd in this place, more fluid than I'm used to somehow. When I finally take my shower, get dressed in my

borrowed skirt and sweater, and go out
to the lobby, Bobby is by the tree, shaking presents. Daniel is behind him,
laughing.

I pause at the corner, watching them.
All it takes is a look at Bobby and
Daniel, a moment in their presence, and
the bitter aftertaste of my previous life is
gone. A smile comes easily; I feel it deep
inside, too, not just a curving of my lips,
but a lifting of my spirit. In some small
way, I have given them this moment.
Without the tree, they wouldn't have
been able to slide back in time, to recap-
ture one of those ordinary moments that
becomes extraordinary from a distance. I
only hope I can do the same for myself.
Stacey and I need to see ourselves more
clearly. Maybe then we can find our
way back.

At the sound of my footsteps, Bobby
looks up. "Joy!" He is shaking a present,
but pauses long enough to say, "Are you
gonna go see the old people with us?"

"What do you mean?"

"Tell 'er where we're goin', Dad."

"The church serves brunch at the nursing home," Daniel answers.

It's what I do on my own holiday. It's a tradition my mom started long ago. For all the years of my childhood, I spent Christmas Eve afternoon at the nursing home with Grandma Lund. In my adult years, I volunteered on holidays.

Fate.

"You better hurry," Daniel says to Bobby and me. I race down to my room, tame my riotous hair, brush my teeth, and make my bed. Then we all go out to the truck.

Between the Christmas lights and the remnants of an early morning rain, the town glistens with water and light. People fill the sidewalks; cars clog the streets.

Daniel pulls into a parking lot and stops. We are at the Rain Shadow Convalescent Center. It's a lovely little brick building set well to the back of a deep lot. A few older trees, bare now, flank the sides, and giant rhododendrons and azaleas grow out front. Christmas lights outline the windows, and a fully lit menorah sits on the sill.

Inside, the center is a hive of activity. In the lobby, several white clad attendants are pushing people in wheelchairs toward a room marked "Christmas Eve Brunch."

"I'll go meet the guys and get breakfast ready. You can help get people to the tables, okay?" Daniel says to us.

"I'll go get Mr. Lundberg!" Bobby cries out, rushing down the hall.

When I turn to ask Daniel something, he's gone, but I don't need his direction. I've spent plenty of time in nursing homes. I know how to help.

I walk down the busy hallway, looking in to the various rooms. Most are empty now. That's why the hallways are so full.

In the very back of the building, I find an elderly woman sitting in a chair, all by herself, facing a window that looks outside. She wears a pale pink ruffled dressing gown, with ribbons in her snow white hair. Her small, heart-shaped face has been overtaken by wrinkles, and bright red lipstick doesn't quite match her lip lines, but her eyes reveal a woman who was once gorgeous enough to stop traffic.

"Hello, there," I say, stepping into the small room. "Merry Christmas Eve. Would you like to go to the brunch?"

She doesn't answer me. I've probably spoken too softly. I enter the room, make my way past the bed, and kneel down in front of her.

She's muttering something, playing with a red satin ribbon. The thin strip of fabric is coiled around her knobby, veiny knuckles.

"Hey," I say, smiling up at her. "I'm here to take you to the brunch." I have to yell the words.

The woman frowns. Her fingers still. She blinks down at me. "Is it my time?"

"The brunch starts in ten minutes."

"My sister is supposed to come for me."

"I'm sure she'll meet you in the dining room." I stand, offer her my hand.

She looks up at me. Her eyes seem huge in her tiny face. "Walk?"

"Let me help you." I help her to her feet and coil my arm around her. It's easy. The woman is almost impossibly frail. Together, moving slowly, we shuffle down the hallway. It's less crowded now. Only a few people are lingering about.

We pass a nurse, or orderly, someone in a white polyester outfit who stares at us, then frowns. "Mrs. Gardiner?"

"It's time to plant tulips," the woman beside me says, tightening her hold on my arm.

We go the last bit to the dining room and turn. At our entrance, I notice how everyone looks up sharply. More than a few gasp. A heavyset nurse rushes toward me. "Mrs. Gardiner, what are you doing here? You know an aide would have brought you a wheelchair."

"She walked really well," I say, holding her steady.

"My sister?" she croaks, looking up at the nurse.

"Now, Mrs. Gardiner, you know Dora is gone. But your son is here, and your granddaughters." The nurse points to a table in the back of the room where a good-looking gray-haired man is seated between a pair of twins. All three of them get to their feet when they see us. Even from here I can see the tears in their eyes.

The man rushes forward, takes his mother's hand. "Hi, Mom." His voice is shaky.

"Where's Dora?" she asks.

"Come on, Mom. Your granddaughters are here." The man tucks her into his side and leads her toward the table.

The nurse beside me shakes her head, makes a tsking sound. "Poor Mrs. Gardiner."

Another nurse joins us, stands beside

me. "She spends all day waiting for her sister."

"It's sad. Dora's been gone almost fifteen years."

I ease away from them and head toward the buffet line to help, but volunteers already stand shoulder to shoulder behind the food.

There's no room for me.

I will do dishes, I guess. I look around for Bobby, but don't see him. From my place in the doorway, I try to get Daniel's attention and fail. He's deep in conversation with an elderly man who seems to want a mountain of hash browns.

I go out into the now-quiet halls. "Bobby?"

When there is no answer, I go in search.

I find him in the recreation room, alone, playing with his action figures. I hear his sound effects before I enter the room.

"Hey, kiddo. What'cha doing?"

He barely looks up at me. "I'm too little."

I sit down on the plaid sofa behind him. "That won't be true for long."

He sits back on his heels. The action figures fall to the side, forgotten. "Mommy never said I was too little. She always let me hand out napkins and stuff."

"Come here, Bobby." I pat the seat beside me. He jumps up to the sofa and snuggles in close. "Did you tell your dad you wanted to help?"

He shakes his head, looking miserable.

"You have to tell people how you feel . . ."

"I'm sorry," Stacey said.

The memory shakes me. Suddenly I have a pounding headache.

I should have listened to her . . .

". . . and give them a chance."

"It's hard," Bobby says.

"You'll get no argument from me on that one, kiddo." Later, when I call my sister, it will be the most difficult thing I've ever done.

Daniel walks in. "There you are. I've been looking all over for you."

I smile at him over Bobby's head. "He was disappointed that he was too little to help serve."

Bobby looks at me for encouragement. At my nod, he turns back to his dad and says quietly, "Mommy always let me help."

"I'm sorry, Bobby. I guess I'm sorta learnin' the ropes on this dad thing."

"That's what Joy said."

Daniel seems surprised by that. "She's a smart woman, your Joy. And now, boyo, it's time for church."

"Oh," Bobby says quietly.

"There's nothing to be afraid of," Daniel says. "I'll hold your hand the whole time. We'll light a candle for your mum. She'd like that."

"You won't let go?" Bobby asks his father.

"I won't," Daniel promises.

Bobby looks at me. "You'll stay with me?"

"Of course."

Bobby takes a deep breath. "Okay," he says. "Let's go."

Awash in light, the church looks like a small white jewel against the royal blue sky.

We stand on the sidewalk out front, Daniel and I, with Bobby between us. All around us, people are talking to one another and funneling up the stone steps to the church.

"Don't let go, Daddy."

"I won't," Daniel says.

They're a pair now, the two of them, holding fast.

Like Dorothy, the Scarecrow, and the Cowardly Lion, we advance cautiously up the sidewalk toward the steps, which we take one at a time.

An elderly priest is positioned at the door. He smiles at the sight of Bobby.

"Welcome back, young Robert," he says, his eyes bright. "We missed you."

Bobby nods in answer and doesn't slow down. I can see how nervous he is, but he keeps moving. One foot in front of the other.

"You're a brave boy," I say, feeling a swell of pride for this child who is learning young to fight his fear.

He leads us into the back row and slides into the pew. I know he wants to be close to the door. Daniel and I book-end him, give him safety on both sides.

As people pour into the church and fill up the pews, Bobby stands as straight as a newly cut board. He doesn't sit until the processional begins and the doors behind us bang shut.

It is then, when the pews are full and the doors are shut and the priest is blessing the congregation, that I realize how much I have missed my own faith. I haven't been in church since my mom's funeral.

For the next hour, we rise and kneel

and rise again, and with each word spoken, each prayer reiterated, I feel a bit of myself return.

At the conclusion of The Lord's Prayer, Bobby looks up at his dad and whispers: "C'n Mommy hear me in here?"

"She can hear you everywhere," Daniel answers.

Bobby scrunches up his face and says, "I'm sorry I was mad at you, Mommy," all in a single breath.

I hear Daniel gasp. "Oh, Bobby . . ."

Bobby's eyes glisten as he looks at his dad. "I told her I hated her."

Daniel touches his son's face, wipes his tears away. "She knows how much you love her, boyo. No silly fight can change that."

The words are exactly what Bobby needs to hear. For the first time, I see his true smile. It lights up his face, shows off all of his crooked, missing, and growing teeth.

When a hymn begins, Bobby turns to

the right page in the hymnal, and joins his clean, high voice with his father's.

For the remainder of the Mass, they stand side by side and hand in hand. I watch them find their voices, and the sight of it fills my heart.

Starting over.

I'm seeing it. For all my dreams of complex new beginnings and convoluted endings, it can all be as easy as this: a boy singing hymns again.

I'm sorry.

I close my eyes at that. When I open them again, the mass is over. People are crowding together, shaking hands, and talking to one another. A ruddy-faced man turns to me, smiling. "How are you today?"

"Fine. Peace be with you." I can't stop smiling. I feel almost giddy with happiness. I'd forgotten this feeling.

We follow the crowd to the parking lot behind the church, where a group of carolers, dressed in old-fashioned Victor-

ian garb, is singing. Volunteers are handing out Styrofoam cups full of hot cider
and paper bags filled with hot nuts.

We stand at the back of the crowd, listening to the beautiful voices.

"I can't see, Dad. Pick me up."

Daniel scoops Bobby into his arms.

I move in close to Daniel. Although
people are all around us, listening to the
carolers, whispering among themselves,
sipping hot cider, I can hear only Daniel's
quiet, even breathing.

The beat of it matches my heart.

And I think: **This is it**. My moment.
If I've learned nothing else in the past
few days, it's that happiness must be
fought for. I need to tell him how I feel
tonight; tomorrow, this adventure of
mine will end. At that, my heart starts
hammering in my chest. A headache
flares behind my eyes. I've always been
afraid to reach for what I want.

But not this time. I won't let a panic
attack stop me.

I turn to him. "Daniel."

The carolers change songs. I recognize the music, but can't quite place the song. Something is wrong. There's a buzzing in my head. My vision is blurring.

"Can you hear me?" I say, making my voice loud. When he doesn't look at me, I dare to touch him. "DANIEL!" I am screaming his name suddenly, trying to grab him.

"Joy?" Bobby is looking at me. "What's wrong?"

I can see how scared he is. And he can see how scared I am.

"Something's wrong," I say. I'm moving away from them, but I don't want to. I fight to get back; there are people everywhere. I think I see Stacey, standing in the crowd. She's crying and saying something, but I can't hear her. But that's not possible. She has no idea where I am.

Something is buzzing. I can hear people talking, yelling.

Don't leave us, Joy.

It's Bobby . . . and it's not.

I reach out, grab Daniel's sleeve. "Help me."

"Dad, help her!"

"Joy?" Daniel whispers my name; at least I think he does. I can't hear anything over the buzzing in my ears.

My chest hurts.

The carolers change songs again. I hear their voices: "It came up-on a Midnight Clear . . ."

CLEAR.

". . . that glor-ious so-ng of old . . ."

CLEAR.

Bobby is reaching for me, screaming. "Joy, you promised. You promised . . ."

CLEAR.

Pain explodes in my chest, rattles my whole body, and the world goes black.

Part Two

"You see things and you say, 'Why?'
But I dream things that never were
And say, 'Why not?'"
—George Bernard Shaw

TEN

*T*he next time I open my eyes, all I see is light, bright white and buzzing.

I am in bed, but it's not my bed in Room 1A. The ceiling overhead is made up of white acoustical tiles with long tubes of fluorescent lighting.

There are people all around me, too, dressed in orange, moving in and out and around me like dancers. I can see them talking to one another, but I can't hear anything except that buzzing in my ears and the **whoosh-thunk** of a machine that sounds like waves breaking on the beach.

On either side of me are machines

that make noises. I see a black television screen with a green graph that moves across it in waves.

I'm in a hospital.

I must have collapsed in the park. Had a heart attack or something. I try to move, to angle up to sit so that I can see more of the room around me, but my arms and legs feel useless, heavy.

"Bobby?" I whisper. My throat burns at the effort. I'm painfully thirsty. "Daniel?"

"Hello, there, Joy. It's nice to see you."

A man's face swims in front of me. I struggle to focus. I can see him in pieces: snow white hair . . . tan skin . . . blue eyes . . . a diamond earring.

It's the man from the gas station.

"Wh . . . t?" I want to ask "what are you doing here?" but my tongue isn't working.

He gives me an ice chip to soothe my fiery throat. "Don't try to talk, Joy. You've been intubated. The soreness in

your throat is normal. I'm Dr. Saunders.
You gave us all quite a scare."

"Who? . . ." **Are you?** I don't understand what's happening and it scares me.

"You just rest now."

The people in my room talk among
themselves in whispered tones designed
to keep me from hearing. Their faces are
a sea of blurry circles; everyone is frowning at me and pointing. There is a lot of
head-shaking going on. One by one,
they leave.

I can hear their footsteps walking
away, and the opening and closing of
a door.

Then there are only the machines
in here with me, making their noises—
a **click-buzz,** a **thunk-whoosh;** a **blip-
blip-blip**. And I am alone, unable to
move, staring up at this unfamiliar
ceiling.

Poor Bobby. He must be terrified.

I won't leave you.

And here I am, in the hospital.

I want him here, beside my bed so that I can smile and tell him I'm fine.

Behind me, the door opens again. Footsteps move haltingly toward me.

It's Bobby. **Thank God.**

I feel a rush of sweet relief. He's knows I didn't leave him. **I'm fine. Fine.** In my head, the protestation is vibrant and clear, but the sound that issues from my cracked, dry lips is barely a whisper and even that useless sound tires me. Instead, I try to lift my hand to show how fine I am.

"Joy?"

It's the wrong voice; not a boy's. It takes forever for me to turn my head, and when I do, the pillow puffs up around my face, blocking the view from my left eye.

I can see well enough, though.

She looks smaller, somehow, like a pencil that's been used down to the nub. Her eyes are swollen and red; there's no mistaking the tear tracks on her cheeks.

Stacey.

I don't understand. How is she here? How did she find me?

"Wha . . . here?"

She leans close, pushing the damp hair from my eyes. Her touch is quick, as if she's not sure it will be welcomed. Almost before I feel it, she draws back. "I was so scared."

"How" **did you** "fin . . ." **me?**

I can see her answering me, but there's something wrong. I can't hear over the buzzing in my ears. My head is pounding, too. I want to ask her where Bobby and Daniel are, but my voice is turning against me. All that comes out is, "Where?"

"They airlifted you to Bakersfield. You're home."

"Home?" The word comes out sounding cracked. I don't understand. **It's Christmas** "Eve?"

"No, I'm sorry. I know how much you love the holidays."

What "Day?"

"It's the thirtieth. You've had a rough

two weeks, but the doctors think you're going to be okay now."

Her words scatter like BBs on a kitchen table; it's impossible to grasp them all at once.

"Daniel?"

Stacey frowns. "Do you understand me, Joy? You were in a plane crash, remember? The firemen rescued you moments before it exploded. The doctors said you might have trouble with your memory."

Rescued you. Firemen.

But I walked away from the crash, left my tattered life behind in the wreckage and went on an adventure. If anyone rescued me, it was Bobby and Daniel. I want to shake my head in denial, but I can't seem to move. "No."

"You were in a medically induced coma for almost ten days. Because of a head injury."

Head injury.

It steals over me like a cold shadow, the meaning of her words. She's saying

I've been here, in this hospital bed, since the crash.

I don't understand. Why would she lie to me? Because I ran away, because I let her think I was dead?

"Joy? What do you remember?"

Daniel and Bobby . . .

Walking away . . .

Dancing by the fire at the beach . . .

My heart starts pounding so fast I can't breathe. Beside me, a machine starts beeping. "Lying," I accuse in a whisper. At the word, and the effort behind it, my throat seems to catch fire.

As if from a distance, I hear my sister calling for someone. Within moments there are people in my room.

I see a needle.

"Quit thrashing," my sister says. "You'll hurt yourself."

Please be lying.

I feel myself fading to gray, closing my eyes. The terrible sound in my head goes still.

Lying.

*   *   *

I'm flying above the rainforest, looking down at the brightly lit tiara of a town. From a great and yawning distance, I see the black ribbon of a road. Moonlight gilds the center line and I follow it.

This time, I know I'm dreaming. I can hear the buzz of the fluorescent lighting overhead and the **thunk-whoosh** sound of the stork-like machine beside my bed. There is also a kind of low-grade thrumming in my blood, a euphoria, that comes from an IV drip. I guess it's camouflaging a serious pain, but it's masking it so well I don't care.

From my place amid the silvery clouds, I see the Comfort Fishing Lodge, tucked down along the glassy gray lake. Moonlight glitters on the water.

That's where I want to be. I close my eyes and make it happen.

When I open my eyes, I'm in the lobby, pressed against the wall. The room is still decorated. The lights of the tree are on; the mantel holds several lit candles amid the snowy town. The stereo is playing Bruce Springsteen's version of "Santa Claus is Coming to Town."

I hear footsteps upstairs. This old place rattles and groans as someone races down the hall overhead, then clatters down the stairs.

It is Bobby. He is at a full Christmas morning run.

At the bottom of the stairs, he pivots left and rushes past me to Room 1A.

He pulls the door open, yelling, "Joy!" and disappears inside.

I picture him skidding to a stop beside the empty bed. The sorrow I feel at that overwhelms me, making it difficult to breathe again.

Daniel comes down the stairs and stops beside me. I long to feel the warmth of him, but I can't. I'm close enough to see the tiny sleep lines that mark his cheek, to hear the soft strains of his breath, and yet I feel as if I'm miles away. "Boyo? I thought you'd go straight to the tree."

Bobby steps back into the hall. He looks smaller somehow, younger. His shoulders are slumped, his mouth is shaking. I can see how hard he is trying not to cry. "She's gone."

I try to go to him, but I can't push away from the wall. My legs are like lead pipes.

Bobby shuffles toward his father in that hangdog way of disappointed children everywhere. "She **promised**. It's just like Mommy."

"I'm here," I say, desperately trying to reach out for him. "Don't say I'm not here."

Daniel pulls Bobby into his arms. I can tell that Bobby is crying, but it's nearly silent, the way of a boy who has learned too early to cry and is trying to hide it.

When Bobby draws back, his eyes are red and watery.

"Remember what the doctor said?" Daniel asks, wiping his son's tears with a gentle hand. "When you didn't need your imaginary friend anymore, she'd leave."

"She wasn't **imaginary**, Dad." He shakes his head. "She **wasn't**. You talked to her."

"The doctors told me to pretend."

I feel as if I've been struck.

I was Bobby's imaginary friend.

Daniel never saw me.

I scream, "It isn't true," but even as I say the words, I remember things. The times Daniel didn't look at me or speak to me. When he **did** talk to me it was a pretense, at doctor's orders, to make Bobby feel loved. Like the time we danced. Now I recall that Bobby pointed to where I was. **She's right there, Daddy. Dance with her.**

"I can be the one you talk to, Bobby," Daniel says. His voice cracks. I can see in his eyes how confused he is by all of this, and how afraid.

"You don't believe me," Bobby says stubbornly. He spins on his heel and marches over to the Christmas tree, then squats in front of it.

At Bobby's movement, I am released. I follow him, move when he does, where he does.

When he kneels at the tree, I sit on the hearth, as I have done so many times before. To my left, the card table is still set up with Candyland. There are three men on the board.

I'll move for Joy, Dad.

At that, another piece clicks into place. Whenever Bobby and I played with action figures, he wanted me to be Frodo, wearing the ring.

The ring that made Frodo invisible.

Bobby reaches underneath the tree and pulls out a small package. It is a crudely wrapped cylinder with ribbons on each end.

We catch our breath at the same time, Bobby and I. It's proof of my impossible journey, isn't it?

"Look, Dad. This is from Joy."

"Bobby . . ."

"Open it."

Daniel takes the cylinder in his hands; it looks tiny and frail against his long, tanned fingers. He unwraps it carefully, extracts the list. As he reads it, he frowns. Then he looks at Bobby. "How did you do this?"

"It's Joy's present to you. She told me what to write."

He glances down at the list again.

I was here.

I was.

Surely Daniel will believe Bobby now.

Daniel looks down at his son. "You did this by yourself," he says quietly. "Please admit it."

"I **couldn't,** Dad," Bobby answers earnestly.

In the silence that follows, Daniel looks around. "Is she here now?"

"No. She disappeared in the park."

"SEE ME," I say as loudly as I can.

Daniel frowns. I can see that he's

bothered by this. He knows Bobby didn't write that list on his own, but he doesn't believe in me. How could he?

"Please believe me," Bobby whispers. "It wasn't like Mommy. Or Mr. Patches. I **swear** it wasn't."

Daniel stares at the list in his hand. The paper shivers a little, as if he's shaking. Then he looks at his son. "You need me to believe in magic."

Bobby's nod brings tears to his father's eyes, and to mine. "Mommy would believe me."

"But . . ."

"Whatever." Bobby sighs. It is a terrible, harrowing sound; in it, I hear his defeat.

At last, Daniel says, "Well, I'm Irish, and we're a crazy lot."

Bobby draws in a sharp breath. It's the sound of hope, this time. "Nana used to say a leprechaun lived in her cookie jar."

Daniel smiles at that. "My point exactly. I guess, boyo, for you I can try to believe, too. But you'll have to show me how."

"Really?"

"Really."

"How do I show you?"

Daniel shrugs. "Tell me about her, I guess. Keep talking until I believe."

Bobby hurls himself into his father's arms.

I see the way Daniel holds his son, with a ferocity that is borne of desperate love. When Bobby draws back, they are both smiling.

See me, I whisper, wanting it so much my chest hurts. **Please.**

"Can we open presents now?"

"Aye."

Bobby runs to the tree and starts dispersing gifts. Most of them collect in a pile on the coffee table. On his last pass, he reaches deep under the tree and pulls out the orange Dr. Seuss book. It has a yellow ribbon stuck dead center. Carrying it carefully, he hands it to his dad, who is now seated on the sofa.

"You're giving me your favorite book, boyo?"

"Nope." Bobby sits down next to Daniel, then opens the book.

"You want me to read to you?" Daniel asks, frowning. "How about . . ."

"Be quiet. I gotta **think**." He scrunches up his face, concentrating hard. One syllable at a time, he sounds out the words. "I . . . am . . . Sam. Sam . . . I . . . am . . ."

"Bobby."

"Sshh, Daddy. 'I . . . do . . . not . . . like . . . green . . . eggs . . . and . . . ham.'"

I listen to Bobby's sweet, stumbling voice, but it is Daniel to whom I look. At first he is sitting upright, in control, but as his son sounds out the words, I see Daniel's control wash away. Everything about him softens—the look in his green eyes, the shelf of his broad shoulders, and the hard line of his spine.

Love. Never have I seen it so clearly or longed for it more desperately.

I'm part of this, I say to them. **See me, too.**

When Bobby finishes the book, he looks up at his dad. "You're cryin'. Did I do bad?"

Daniel touches his son's cheek. "Your mum would be so proud of you."

Tears sting my eyes, make everything blurry, and I'm glad. I need this moment to be out of focus.

"Joy taught me every day."

Daniel stares down at his son for a long moment. "Did she now? Then I guess your Joy has a place here, doesn't she?"

"I miss her, Dad."

"I know, but you've got your old man, and he's not going anywhere."

"You promise?"

I can hear the fear in Bobby's voice, and in the sound, I make sense of it all. That's been Bobby's fear all along. That he would be alone. It was the same fear that caused me to board the airplane bound for Hope.

"I promise."

I lean forward. It is as much movement as I can make. "Believe in me," I say desperately, willing them to see with their hearts. I focus all my mind on it, thinking over and over again: **Believe.**

The effort takes everything I have. When I'm done, I can hardly breathe. I feel my heartbeat speed up again. The world starts to go fuzzy and out of focus.

I am fading.

Fading.

I reach out for something to hold on to.

There's nothing. I close my eyes and scream: **No!**

When I open my eyes again, I see bright white lights. A nurse is standing by my bed. It is the woman I "met" at the doctor's office in my dream.

"How are we today?" she asks in her completely familiar voice.

"I'm fine," I manage, closing my eyes again. I try to find my way back to the rainforest, but, this time, all I see is darkness.

I want to be on the drugs again.

Instead, I am fully awake now, and sitting up in bed. There are so many people clustered around me that I can't see the walls behind them. A sheen of light hugs the ceiling, coming from a window I can't see.

I find myself listening for the rain.

But I am in Bakersfield now; it's the thirty-first of December, and the sun is shining outside.

"I don't understand what you're saying. Tell me again."

The people gathered around me frown. I recognize all of them. There's Stacey, of course. She hasn't left the room since I woke up, except to go out for food or—no doubt—to call Thom. And the nurse I saw in my dream. She's the day nurse who has been taking care of me. The ruddy-faced man from church is the orthopedist who put my right leg back together. Apparently I'm held together by a titanium pin of some kind. This is more than I can say for my mind, which is held together lately by nothing. The gas station guy is my cardiologist; he brought me back to life, though the real credit goes to a man and boy who probably don't exist.

"Your right leg was broken just below the knee. And your concussion was quite severe. We worried about swelling of the brain for several days," says the gas station attendant, whom I now have to start calling Dr. Saunders.

I want to make a joke about having a bigger brain, but words fail me.

"With a little physical therapy, you'll be fine," my sister says. The council nods in unison like bobbleheads in the back-seat of a car.

"Can I still ice skate?" I ask, although I haven't ice skated since Melinda Carter's ninth birthday party.

Dr. Saunders frowns. This is a question he didn't anticipate. "In time, certainly, but . . . "

"Never mind." I try to smile. "When can I go home?"

The head bobbing starts again. This is a question they like. "You'll have to take it easy for a while," says Dr. Saunders.

I look down at my casted right leg. No kidding.

"But if you're careful, and barring any unforeseen complications, we think you can go home in a few days."

I want to smile for them. I really do. I know how hard they have all worked to help me so that I can go home.

Alone. "That's great."

I see how Stacey looks at me. She knows what I'm thinking. It is a bond that has been in place a long time, and apparently neither anger nor betrayal can break it.

"Thanks," I say, meaning it.

As a group, they leave, and we are left alone, Stacey and I.

Neither one of us speaks. We obviously don't know what to say, how to start.

It's up to me; I know that. She has already made her move—she invited me to her wedding. It's why I'm lying here, hooked up to machines and held together by a metal pin.

I sit up, reposition the pillows. The minute I'm up here, I know it's a mistake. There's no way to avoid seeing Stacey's stomach. She has gained a few pounds already.

She notices where I'm looking. "I'm surprised you haven't thrown me out," she says, softly. I can hear the longing in her voice, the missing of me, and it reminds me of a dozen memories of our youth.

"At your current weight, I'd need some kind of catapult."

She wants to smile at my lame joke; I can see the desire. But she doesn't. Probably she can't. Neither can I. "I haven't gained that much."

"If I had two good legs, I'd kick your ass, though."

"Stop," Stacey says. "You always make jokes when you're hurting."

And there it is: the core of everything. We're sisters. We know each other intimately. Our pasts, our secrets, our fears. It is a precious gift that we tried to throw away but can't really let go of.

Stacey bites her lower lip. It's what she's done her whole life when she's scared. "I'm sorry, Joy. I don't know how it happened. I didn't mean . . ."

I hold up my hand. Of all the things we could say now, the hows and whys of what happened are at the bottom of my list. But I make my move too late; her words get through, make me angry . . . and hurt me. "You make it sound like you slipped on a banana peel and fell on my husband."

"So what do we do?"

The soft tenor of her voice, the trembling of her lip, the regret in her eyes; I see it all, and in seeing it, seeing **her,** I lose that spark of anger, just let it go. When the plane was going down, it was Stacey whom I thought about. That's what I need to always remember now. "We find a way to get past it. That's all."

"Who are you and what have you done with my sister?"

"Now who's trying to be funny?"

Stacey stares down at me with a combination of awe and gratitude. "Two weeks ago you hated me."

"I never hated you, Stace," I say the words softly, realizing almost before I've finished that they're not enough. What I want to say, need to say, now before I lose my nerve is what I learned in the rainforest: "We're sisters."

At that, Stacey starts to cry.

I wait for her to say something, but she remains quiet. Maybe, like me, she's wondering how exactly we move forward from here. "It won't be easy," I say.

She wipes her eyes. "What is?" Taking a small step closer, she looks down at me, pushes a strand of hair from my eyes. "I **am** sorry, you know."

"I know." I sigh. "When I was in the rainforest," I stop abruptly, realizing what I was about to say.

"What rainforest?"

I try to smile and fail. "If I told you, you'd think I was brain damaged. Or crazy."

"You're the most level-headed person I know."

I look at her closely, trying to gauge how much to say. "On television, I heard you tell the reporters you were hoping I'd come back to you."

Stacey frowns. "How—?"

"Just answer me. Did you say that?"

"I did. I prayed every day that you'd wake up and come back."

Somehow, I saw that real broadcast from a fake world. "And you were wearing the yellow outfit I bought you."

Stacey nods slowly, then leans forward, rests her arms on the rail. "You never saw that broadcast. You were in a coma."

Who can I tell if not my sister? And I **need** to tell someone. I'm like the "I see dead people" kid. If I try to handle this all alone, I'll go nuts. "After the crash, I woke up . . ."

She shakes her head. "No. You never regained consciousness. The paramedics . . ."

"Crazy, remember?"

"Oh."

"Anyway, I was in this clearing. There was smoke everywhere, and fire, and loud noises, and . . . Mom."

Stacey goes very still. "You saw her?"

I nod.

"And?"

"She knelt beside me and told me it wasn't my time." I lean forward slightly, desperate to be told I'm not insane, even though I know I must be. "Tell me I'm wacko."

"In the field . . . Your heart stopped for almost a minute. You were legally dead."

I release a deep breath. There's a strange sense of peace that comes with the news. "She made me wake up. When I did, I saw how alone I was, how far from the survivors. At first, I was going to go to them and get rescued, then I thought of you and I changed my mind. I walked away from the crash and ended up in some little town in Washington."

"You know the plane crashed about one hundred miles northeast of here?"

It shakes me, that new bit of information. "I was never even in Washington State?"

"No."

I'll think about that later. For now, since I've started on my mad story, I want to finish it. "I found a run-down resort called The Comfort Fishing Lodge and got a room. There was a boy there, and a man."

Stacey holds up a hand to stop me. "Wait a second." She runs to the corner of the room, where my purse is on a mustard-yellow plastic seat. Beside it is my camera.

"My camera," I whisper. "Did you develop my film?"

"Huh? No." Stacey digs through my black leather tote and finally pulls out a magazine, then hurries back to my side. "I read this while you were in surgery." She opens it to a page, hands it to me.

It's the article on The Comfort Fishing Lodge. "I was looking at this in the airport."

I feel as if I'm unraveling, coming apart. **This** is where it began. In my subconscious. I looked at the pictures of this place and longed to go there. And a morphine drip made it possible.

"This article says the lodge was torn down in 2003, to make way for a corporate retreat."

Torn down.

"Does it mention a Daniel?"

Stacey scans the pages. "No. The resort was built by Mr. and Mrs. Melvin Hightower. They moved to Arizona when the Zimon Corporation purchased it. The new place hosts corporate shindigs and self-help seminars."

There is no Comfort Fishing Lodge.

I was never there.

No doubt Daniel is my neurologist and Bobby is some nurse's son who darted into my room for a second while I was sleeping.

"Joy, are you okay?"

I close my eyes so she won't see my tears. "No."

"You're scaring me."

I finally look at her. Through my tears, I can see how worried she is. I wish I could reassure her, but I can't. "Will you develop my film?"

"Are you sure you want me to?"

I sigh. "Stace, I'm not sure about anything."

ELEVEN

I am like an autistic with a puzzle. For the rest of my hospital stay, I study the pieces, putting them together in a dozen ways in an attempt to see the whole picture.

They tell me I didn't walk away from the crash and I don't believe they're lying.

I've seen the newspaper stories—complete with photographs that made me physically ill. Several of the passengers, including Riegert, reported seeing me carried off the plane. As soon as they found my purse and identification, they called Stacey. I may be brain damaged and hallucinatory and drug addled, but I'm not stupid. I can add up the evidence.

I never walked away from the crash.

That's what I know.

Somehow I have to make it what I believe.

If I could **remember** the crash, maybe that would make everything real. But the shrinks who now circle me like sharks in bloody water, think I'll never remember. "Too traumatic," they say.

I tell them "remembering" Daniel and Bobby hurts me more.

They don't like that, the brain experts. Whenever I mention my adventure, they make tsk-tsk sounds and shake their heads.

Only Stacey lets me talk about Bobby and Daniel as if they're real, and that—the simple act of her silent acceptance—somehow draws us together again. It seems, after all, that I am not the only one who has been changed by my near death. The nurses tell me that Stacey was my champion throughout it all, demanding the best for me, and organizing prayer and candlelight vigils in town.

Last night, she even slept in my room; this morning, she was up at the crack of dawn, readying my discharge papers.

"Are you ready to go?"

Now she is standing by the door. A nurse is next to her, with an empty wheelchair.

"I'm ready."

I could knit a sweater in the time it takes me to get out of bed and into the wheelchair.

No one seems to notice but me. And then we are off, tooling down the hallway. Everyone I see says: "Good bye, Joy. Good luck." I mumble thanks and try to look happy about going home.

Outside, Stacey rolls me over to a brand-new red minivan.

"New car, huh?"

"Thom got it for me for Christmas," she says.

Thom. It is the first time she's said his name to me.

We stare at each other for an uncomfortable moment longer, then she helps me into the passenger seat.

On the drive home we try to find things to say, but it isn't easy. Suddenly, it's as if my ex-husband is in the backseat, scenting the air between us with his aftershave.

"I got your car from the airport," Stacey says as she turns onto Mullen Avenue.

It seems like a year ago that I turned into the long-term parking area. "How was the tree? Did it catch fire on the drive home?"

"The tree was fine. I donated it to the nursing home on Sunset."

That's right. The tree was only strapped onto my car for a day or so. Not the week I imagined. "Thanks."

Stacey pulls into my driveway and parks. "You're home."

There are cars everywhere, and lights are on all up and down the street, but the neighborhood is strangely silent for late afternoon. For almost ten years I have lived in this house, on this street, and yet, just now, looking at it, I wonder if it ever really was my home. Rather, it was where I passed the time between shifts at the high school and tried to make a failing marriage into something it could never be.

The Comfort Lodge . . .

(which doesn't apparently exist)

. . . now that's a home.

Don't go there, Joy.

Stacey comes around to my door and helps me out. She gets me situated on my crutches and together, moving slowly, we make our way around the yard.

We are at the corner, by the huge, winter-dead lilac tree that was our first investment in the yard, when a crowd of people surge out from behind the house, yelling, "Surprise!"

I stumble to a halt. Stacey places a hand in the small of my back to steady me.

There must be two hundred people in front of me; most are holding lit candles, several hold up signs that say "Welcome Home, Joy." The first person to come forward is Gracie Leon—a girl I suspended last semester for defacing all three copies of **To Kill a Mockingbird**. "We prayed for you, Mrs. Candellaro."

A young man comes forward next, stands beside Gracie. Willie Schmidt. Seven years ago, he was my fourth period teacher's assistant. Now he has students of his own at a local high school. "Welcome back," he says, handing me a beautiful pink box. Inside it are hundreds of cards.

Mary Moro is next. She's a junior this year, and head cheerleader. She holds out a Christmas cactus in a white porcelain bowl. "I bought this with my babysitting money, Mrs. Candellaro. Remember when you said the only plant you could keep alive was a cactus?"

Then I see Bertie and Rayla from work; they stand pressed together like a pair of salt and pepper shakers. Both of them have left their families to be here.

My throat is so full I can hardly nod. It's all I can do to whisper, "Thanks."

They surge toward me, all talking at once.

We stand in the yard, talking and laughing and sharing the surface connections of our lives. No one mentions the plane crash, but I feel their curiosity; unasked questions hang behind other words. I wonder if and when it will become a thing I can talk about.

By the time they finally start to leave, night is falling on Madrona Lane. The streetlamps are coming on.

My sister guides me to my front door and unlocks it.

My house, on my return, is as silent as it was when I left.

"I put you in the downstairs bedroom," Stacey says, and our thoughts veer onto an ugly road. We are both remembering the day I came home to find her in my bed.

It is not the first time our thoughts have gone here and it won't be the last. Our recent past is like a speed bump; you slow down and go over it, then drive on your way again.

"Good thinking," I say.

She helps me get settled in the downstairs guest room. When I'm in bed, she brings me several books, a plate of cheese and crackers, a Big Gulp from the local mini mart, the television remote and my wireless laptop. I notice a magazine in with the books. It's the same **Redbook** I was reading in the lodge. "That's pretty old," I say, pointing to it.

Stacey glances at the magazine, then shrugs. "I read it to you in the hospital almost every day. There was a great article in it on refurbishing a log cabin that used to be a bed and breakfast. Remember when you wanted to be an innkeeper?"

"Yeah," is all I can say. No wonder my Comfort Lodge was in need of repair.

Stacey props my cast onto a pillow, then steps back. "Will you be okay for the night? I could stay."

"No. Your . . . Thom will miss you."

"He wants to see you."

"Does he? That's quite a turn around."

We stare at each other; neither of us knows where to go after that.

"It's like napalm, the way it comes and goes," Stacey says.

"Yeah."

"I can stay."

"Go home to your . . ." Despite my best intentions, I trip up. What do I call him, my ex-husband? Her lover? Boyfriend? What?

"Fiancé." She stares at me hard, biting her lip. I know she wants to say just the right thing, as if the perfect words are a bleach that can remove this stain between us.

The silence lingers, turns awkward. I want to mention her wedding, perhaps even say I'll be there, but I don't know if I dare promise such a thing.

I can see how the quiet between us wounds her. She tries valiantly to smile. "Did you tell Mom about me and Thom, by the way?"

"You think that's what was on my mind when I was dying?"

"You always were a tattletale."

I can't help smiling at that. Her words take us back to a time when there was no silence between us. Suddenly we're six and seven again, fighting in the smelly backseat of Mom's VW bus. "You're right. And, yes, I told her."

"What did she say?"

"She told me to wake up. It's good advice."

Stacey reaches out, brushes the hair from my eyes. "When you were . . . sleeping, I didn't think I'd get another chance with you."

I don't know what to say except, "I know." The nurses have told me that her devotion to me was legendary.

"I was there at the hospital, you

know," she says. "From the second we heard. I almost never left."

It's what I would have done for her, too. "I missed you, Stace."

She finally smiles. "I missed you, too."

By the end of my first week at home, I'm ready to scream.

I spend the better part of my days on pain pills, trying not to move. Everything hurts, but pain is not the worst of it. What I hate most are the nights.

I lie in bed, staring up at my ceiling, trying to tell myself that the rainforest was a construct of my own mind. Before the plane crash, I was lost and lonely, desperate to **want** someone and be wanted in return. I can admit it now; losing both my sister and my husband unhinged me somehow. Without them, I was adrift.

So I made up the man I wanted to love me and the boy I wanted to love.

In the cold light of day, it makes sense.

I was tired of hot, dry Bakersfield; I imagined a magical world of green grass and towering trees and impossible mist.

On paper, it pencils out, makes perfect sense in a psych 101 kind of way. At night, however, it's different.

Then, the darkness—and my loneliness—just goes on and on and on. For the first time in my life, I can't read to pass the time. Every hero becomes Daniel; every heartfelt moment makes me sob. Even movies are useless. When I turn on the television I remember **Miracle on 34th Street** and the Grinch; not to mention the fifteen Winnie-the-Pooh videos we watched.

God help me, in the darkness, I believe. Over and over again, I try to "return." Each attempt and failure diminishes my hope.

I can't stand it.

It's time for me to either fish or cut bait. I've spent too long floating on a drug sea, dreaming of one place, and sitting in another. I need to believe in my rainforest, to find it, or to let it go. It's a cinch what my shrink would advise. There's no room in the real world for the kind of fantasy realm I've imagined. But I keep thinking of moments—the way Daniel and I said "fate" at the same time; the way our wish on the star was the same. The television broadcast with Stacey. I didn't hear her broadcast from my coma; I saw it. And there's the fix-it list Bobby had on Christmas morning. Maybe that was somehow real. If it was, I was there, however impossible that sounds.

What I need is evidence. And if there's one thing a librarian can do, it's research.

Throwing the covers back, I hobble out of bed, get my crutches and then turn on all the lights. In the garage, I find what I'm looking for: my files. I take several—the Pacific Northwest, Washington, and North American rainforests. Clutching the manila folders to my side, I return to the desk in my living room.

Beneath a light bright enough to dis-

pel shadows and sharp enough to illuminate the truth, I begin laying out my ma-
terials, organizing them into piles. Then I
turn on my laptop and search the Web.

It doesn't take long to identify the core
problem.

All I know about my dream life is that
it took place in a rainforest in Washington State. According to a Googled sta-
tistic, the Olympic National Forest is
roughly the size of Massachusetts.

And I am trying to find one—
imaginary—lakeside town that probably
has a population of less than one thousand people.

Oh, and let's not forget that I don't
know the name of the town, or the lake,
or Daniel and Bobby's last name.

A woman less impressionable might
say that if fate exists, it doesn't want me
to find my way back.

Still, I trudge ahead, unwilling—
unable, maybe—to give up. I make my
own map, underline possible towns and
lakes and call information for each city I

can find. There is no listing for a
Comfort Fishing Lodge. Then I call real-
tors. There are two fishing lodges for sale
in the area; I've gotten e-mail photos of
both. Neither is the one I remember.

Finally, nearly eight hours after I begin
my search, I shut my laptop and lay my
head on top of it, closing my eyes. By
now, the walls of my living room are
studded with pieces of paper—maps,
photographs, articles. The place looks
like a task force command center.

And none of it helps.

I don't know exactly how long I remain there. At some point, I hear a car
drive up.

I glance up, and see Stacey's van pull
into the driveway.

I grab my crutches and head for
the entry.

At her first knock, I open the door.

She is on my porch, holding a casserole pan in gloved hands.

It's Mom's chicken divan recipe.
Chicken, cheese, mayonnaise, and broc-

coli. "I guess you forgot about them re-starting my heart."

Stacey pales. "Oh. I didn't . . ."

"I'm just kidding. It looks great. Thanks." I wobble around and make my way back to the living room.

Stacey veers into the kitchen, probably puts the casserole in the oven, and then joins me. In the living room, she comes to a dead stop. Her gaze moves from wall to wall, where papers hang in grape-like bunches.

"Welcome to Obsessionville," I say. There's no point in trying to explain. I make my halting way to the sofa and sit down, planting my casted foot on the coffee table. "I'm searching for the town."

"The one you never went to."

"That's the one."

Stacey sits in the chair opposite me. "I'm worried about you. Thom says . . ."

"Let's not start a conversation like that. It's your turn to care about what he says."

"You've been home almost seven days and you haven't let anyone visit except me. And now . . ." She lifts her hand to indicate the walls. "This."

"Bertie and Rayla have both stopped by."

Stacey gives me "The Look." "Bertie called me because you said you were too tired to see her."

"I'm in **pain**."

"Is that really it?"

"What are you, my keeper?" I don't want to explain the inexplicable.

"It's that dream, isn't it?"

I sigh, feeling my defenses crumble. All I can tell her now is the sad truth. "I can't let go of it. I know it's crazy—that I'm crazy—but the pictures are so familiar. I know how it smells there and **feels** there, how the mist floats up from the grass in the morning. How do I know these things? Maybe when you develop my film, I'll get an answer." It's the dream I've clung to.

As I say the words, I see my sister

frown. It's a quick expression, there and gone, but if there's one thing sisters recognize in each other, it's a secret being kept. "What?"

"What what?"

"You're hiding something from me, and, given that your last big secret was my husband, I'm . . ."

Stacey stands. Turning away, she walks out of the room. A few moments later she's back, carrying a manila envelope. "Here."

I take it from her, though if I had two good legs, my instinct is to run. "I won't like this, will I?"

"No." Stacey's voice is soft; that makes me more nervous.

I open the envelope and find photographs inside. I look up at Stacey, who shakes her head.

"I'm sorry."

The envelope drops from my grasp. I turn through the pictures. When I get to the few taken in the airport, I gasp.

There's the plane, before the crash, and the crowd of hunters waiting to board, and the interior before takeoff. Riegert, giving his buddy the thumbs up.

After that, nothing.

No photos of the lodge or the rainforest or the lake. No spiderwebs dripping with dew, no clusters of old growth trees and the giant ferns at their feet. Just twenty-nine empty gray pictures.

"I wasn't there," I say slowly, feeling it for the first time.

"I'm sorry, Joy," Stacey says after a moment, "but you have a real life here. And people who love you. Rayla says students ask about you every day."

I can hear my sister talking, but the words are like smoke, drifting past me. All I can think about is the boy who made me promise to stay for Christmas. My heart feels like it's breaking down the middle; it's hard to breathe. It takes all my self-control not to cry at the smoky, blank photographs. Still, I know what

I'm supposed to say, what she wants to hear. "I'm sure everything will be fine when I start working again."

"Don't you miss it?'

It takes me a minute to hear her. I look up. "Miss what?"

"The library. You used to love it."

I know Stacey hears herself say **love it;** all I hear is **used to**. "What I love doesn't seem to exist."

"You're starting to scare me."

"Join the club, little sister."

It is amazing how quickly a bone can heal. If only the heart were as durable. A little plaster, two months of bed rest, and **voila!** your broken heart is mended. I wish it were true.

By late February, I am moving well again. My headaches are all but gone and my leg is coming along nicely, according to the battalion of doctors who oversee my care. They urge me to consider returning to work, though, to be honest, I have trouble contemplating my future.

It's because of the nights.

Alone in my bed, I can't control or corral my thoughts. In sleep, I dream about the Comfort Lodge and Daniel and Bobby.

Even during the stark, bright daylight hours, I have problems. No matter what I'm supposed to be doing, I keep drifting northward in my mind. Everything reminds me of the pseudo-memories I can't let go of.

My psychiatrist—the newest member of the post-crash-save-Joy-team tells me that what I've experienced is not that uncommon. Apparently lots of head cases are head cases, if you know what I mean.

My shrink says it's because I'm not happy with my real life. She thinks I've let the accident paralyze me emotionally, and that when I wake up, I'll quit needing a forest mirage as my ideal.

I tell her she's wrong. I was emotionally paralyzed **before** the crash. This is just same old–same old. The difference is, now I know what I want. I just can't find it.

Before the crash, I wanted Thom back. Now I'm actually happy he's gone. I worry for my sister that it's dangerous to love a man who has already betrayed one wife, but she has made her choice, and truthfully, at his heart, Thom is a good man. I can only hope he'll be a good husband to my sister.

I'm so deep in thought, I'm surprised when I hear my doorbell ring.

I glance at the clock. It's twelve-fifteen. As usual, she's right on time with my lunch. "Come in," I say, getting to my feet, reaching for the crutches.

Stacey comes in, carrying a stack of magazines and videos. They have become her peace offerings, these things she collects for me, her way of saying she doesn't think I'm crazy, even though I'm sure she does. "These are the newest **Sunset** magazines—two have articles on rainforest getaways—four local Sunday newspapers, and two movies shot up there. **Harry and the Hendersons,** about a Sasquatch, and **Double Jeopardy.**"

We both know how much it means to me, these pointless, silly gifts; we also know it won't do any good. I'm not going to suddenly "see" where I've imagined. The walls of my downstairs are now entirely covered with maps and photographs. None of the butter yellow walls beneath can be seen.

I take the pile of things from Stacey, knowing I will watch or read each item carefully. Knowing, too, that all I'll find are images that strike a chord but create no real memory.

While Stacey puts things away in the kitchen, I go into my living room and sit down on the sofa. In the new **Sunset** magazine, I see a photograph of the Hoh rainforest that makes me feel homesick for a place that doesn't exist.

"Joy?"

I look up to see Stacey holding a tray

of croissant sandwiches. It isn't until I see the look on her face that I realize I'm crying.

"Maybe I shouldn't bring you this stuff."

"I need them," I hear the panicked edge in my voice.

So does she. She sets the tray down on the coffee table. "You have to come into the real world." Her voice is tentative; I know she's wanted to say this for a long time, but has been afraid. We are not yet the sisters we once were, who could say anything to each other. She plucks up a sandwich, sets it on a napkin and sits across from me.

"The real world," I say softly, putting the magazine aside. Getting up, I make my awkward way to the window. There I stand on my good leg, staring out at the houses across the street. Now, in the winter, the lawns are dead and brown, as are the trees. There hasn't been a leaf on the road for months. Everything on the block is gray or brown, it seems, and the pale sunlight only manages to dull it all. "Last night I dreamt I was stuck right here," I say, without turning to look at Stacey. "Watching life pass me by. In my dream, I could see your house. Your lights were always on; there were kids in your yard. One of them was a quiet, watchful girl who always waited her turn. You named her Joy. And here I was, stuck. Wrinkling like a dying grape, going gray, wanting." I take a deep breath and turn around to face her. There's something I need to tell her; something I probably should have admitted before. "You weren't the only reason I got on that plane. Most of it, maybe, but not all. I was so tired of who I'd become."

Stacey doesn't respond to that. I'm not surprised. She doesn't know what to say, and she doesn't want to say the wrong thing. Our relationship is fragile; we both handle it like hot glass.

"You can't understand," I finally say.

How could she? My sister never let anything pass her by. She's never been a spectator.

"Are you kidding?" She stares at me as if I am a science exhibit under glass. "You think I don't know about wanting more?"

"You were a cheerleader, for gosh sake, and homecoming queen. And now you're pregnant and in love."

"Sixteen years ago I was a cheerleader, Joy. When you went off to college, I stayed in Bakersfield and worked dead-end jobs."

"But you met Chris . . ."

"And he didn't just break my heart, he shattered it, remember?" She sighs. "I used to watch your life and feel like such a failure. You came home from college in love with Thom and had the perfect wedding and then got the great job at the high school. You succeeded at everything you tried. I hated always being in your shadow."

I frown. "Is that why you moved away?"

"I thought a big city would help, but
in Sacramento I felt even more lost. It
was too busy for me. So I came back here
and used my divorce settlement to buy a
house, but I still couldn't manage to get
a decent job. It's tough when you're
twenty-eight years old with no husband
and no education—especially when your
sister seems to have it all."

"You should have come to me."

"I tried."

I want to tell her it's not true, but we're
well past the lying-to-each-other stage.
The last year has given us that, at least. I
glance out the window; anything is better
than looking at her. "I know you did, but
I was barely hanging on. Thom and I
were fighting like crazy."

"I know," she says softly. "I came over
one day to talk to you, and found him
at home."

So that's how it had begun. I'd wanted
to know, though I never would have
asked. Now that she's planted the words,
I see them grow: how they were friends

first, my sister and my husband, commiserating about their disappointed lives, then commiserating about me, then finding solace in each other.

"It took him a long time to tell me how unhappy he was, but once he did . . ."

I hold up my hand. "I get it."

"So, I know about being lost, Joy," she says instead. "Can you imagine how it feels to hurt the one person you love most in the world? To break your sister's heart and know you can never apologize enough?"

This time when I look at my sister I see a woman I've never met, one who's been through hard times—is still going through them, perhaps—and lives with the pain of her own bad choices. She knows about fading; maybe every woman of a certain age does, especially in quiet towns like this one where the sun can be so hot.

Not like the rainforest.

There, in that moist green and blue

world, there is no drying up of a woman's spirit.

I push that thought away. No good can come of it. I turn back to Stacey. This is what matters. Us. Whatever is unreal about who I met or where I've been, it's all led me back to this moment with my sister. The beginning. "So," I say softly, "how's the pregnancy going?"

I hear her surprise; she takes a thin breath and battles a sudden smile. I can't help wondering how long she's been waiting for me to ask. "Good. The doctors say everything is normal."

"Do you know if it's a boy or a girl?"

"They think it's a girl."

A niece to shop for; dress up like a little doll . . . love. "Mom would have gone nuts."

"We thought we'd name her Elizabeth Sharon."

That hits me hard. "Yeah. She'd like that."

We fall silent again. I want to say more, make a sweet, innocuous comment about the baby, but I've lost my voice. Selfishly, I am caught in my own sense of loss; I take a deep breath and try to let it go, but it's difficult. I keep remembering my dream, where I was frozen in this spot, the aging aunt, watching life pass her by.

"You're losing it, aren't you?" Stacey says after the pause.

I look at her, wondering if that's accurate. Can you lose something you never really had? "I'm scared, Stace. It's like . . . I don't know what to hang on to. I feel like I'm going crazy."

She stares at me, frowning. Just when I expect an answer, she leaves the room. I hear her making a phone call in the kitchen. Then she returns and says, "Come on. I'm taking you somewhere."

"Where?"

"What do you care? It's out of this house. Get your purse."

To be honest, I'm thankful for the distraction. I follow her out to the minivan.

Fifteen minutes later, we pull up to our destination.

The high school is bathed in lemony sunlight. Bright purple crocuses cover the dry brown ground around the flagpole, reminding me that spring is on its way.

"Are you okay?"

It is a question I've come to hate. To answer it requires either a lie or a truth that no one—me included—wants to hear.

"Why are we here?"

"Because it's where you belong."

"Is it?"

Stacey says something I can't quite hear, then gets out of the van and slams the door.

I get out of the minivan and stand on the sidewalk, leaning heavily on my crutches. Gripping their padded handles, I step-swing-step-swing down the wide cement courtyard toward the administrative building.

The Quad is surprisingly quiet today,

no kids skipping classes to play hacky sack in the sunshine or looking for a place to kiss or smoke.

Stacey runs ahead to the building and opens the door for me. Familiar flyers— they're the same ones year after year— clutter the bulletin boards in the hallway. They're looking for student leaders, and singers for this year's spring musical, and volunteers willing to decorate for the up- coming dance.

As I approach the main entrance, the bell rings. Within seconds, the Quad is crowded with kids laughing and talking.

When they see me, a roar of recogni- tion goes up. Suddenly I'm Mick Jagger on stage. A star. Everyone talks to me at once, crowding in close.

Stacey squeezes my arm. "This," she whispers in my ear, "is your real life."

It takes us the entire ten minutes of the class break to work our way through the crowd and to the main office, where we're overwhelmed again. Finally, when I've hugged at least one hundred people and been welcomed back by even more, we make our way down the hall to the library.

I'm struggling with my crutches at the turnstile, when I hear Rayla's throaty laughter and scratchy, I-used-to-be-a-Camel-unfiltered-smoker's voice. "Well, it's about darn time."

I push through the shiny metal barrier and find her standing at the checkout desk, with a skyscraper of books beside her elbow. "This is a big job for one woman," she says with a toothy grin.

I laugh at that. We both know that either of us could easily do it alone. It is a secret we keep from the administration. "Now, Rayla, you know you love bossing the kids around when I'm gone."

She comes around the desk, her skirt flowing, her silver bracelets tinkling, and enfolds me in a fierce hug that smells of hairspray and Tabu perfume. "We missed you, kiddo," she says.

I draw back, look down at her. "I've missed you, too." And it's true.

For the next half hour, we walk around the library, talking about ordinary things—budget cuts, contract negotiations, recent acquisitions, and Rayla's upcoming spring break trip to Reno.

"So," she says at last. "When can we expect you back?"

It is the question I've been dreading. **Back.** By definition, it's a return to what was.

I take a deep breath, knowing there is only one acceptable answer, only one sane one.

Stacey is watching me closely. So is Rayla. They both know. Not everything, perhaps, not all the reasons for my disquiet and my disappointment, but enough.

"Soon," I say, trying to smile.

On the drive home, Stacey and I are quiet.

I feel like Dorothy, back in Kansas, a

black-and-white girl in a black-and-white world, with memories in color.

Beside me Stacey sings along to some catchy, generic song from one of the American Idol runners-up.

Then it's Bruce Springsteen, singing "Baby, I Was Born to Run."

Memory overwhelms me. I close my eyes, remembering.

I'm in a red truck, bouncing down a country road, singing along to the radio. I can feel Bobby beside me, hear him laughing.

When I open my eyes—unable to take any more—I see the airport exit.

It can't be accidental. Stacey never goes home this way.

And I think: Dorothy had to click her heels together three times and say, "There's no place like home." Even magic requires **something.**

Maybe I need to quit waiting for proof and go in search of Hope, like I did before. "Turn here, Stacey."

"You were never there." I know how much she hates to say those words to me. It's in her voice. "You saw your real life at the high school."

"Please?"

With a sigh, she follows the exit to the airport and pulls up outside the America West ticket counter. "This is crazy, Joy."

"I know." I grab my purse and the crutches from the backseat, and I'm off, hobbling into the terminal. At the counter, I find a beautiful dark-haired woman in a blue and white uniform. Her nametag identifies her as Donna Farnham.

"May I help you?"

"I want a ticket to Seattle on the next flight."

The ticket agent looks to her computer screen, types quickly on the keys, then looks up at me. "There's a flight leaving in forty minutes. The next one is tomorrow afternoon. Same time."

I reach into my purse for my wallet. What's a credit card for if not unnecessary expenditures? "I'll take a ticket for today."

"All we have left is first class."

I don't even ask how much. "Great. I'll take it."

By the time I've made it through the security line and find my way to the gate, my hands are sweating and my heart is hammering.

I try to think of Daniel and Bobby, try to believe I can make the magic strike again. **I'm Dorothy. There's no place like home,** I tell myself, but my confidence is draining fast, being pummeled by the bright fluorescent lights overhead. In this light, I can't help seeing clearly.

When they call my flight, I take a step forward.

Then I see the plane.

Images charge me; hit me so hard I almost fall down. I close my eyes and try to breathe, but that's no help. In the darkness, I'm on the plane again, going down. Flames are all around me . . . I smell the stink of fuel . . . and hear the screams.

I'm falling, tumbling, and hitting . . . being carried out of the wreckage. I can see it all: my face covered with blood; my arm hanging down from the gurney; the bone poking up through my torn, bloody jeans. The plane exploding behind me.

The shaking starts in my fingers and radiates outward until I can hardly hold onto my crutches. My palms are slick with sweat; I can't swallow. Tears stream down my cheeks and blur my vision. Several people ask if I'm okay. I nod and push them away. If I could run, I would, but I'm as broken outside right now as I feel within, so I leave slowly, limping away from Hope. I'd crawl if I had to.

When I finally emerge from the terminal and step out into the bright, sunlit day, I see my sister.

She's standing in front of her minivan, by the passenger door.

I go to her, clutching my ticket. "I remember."

She puts her arms around me, holds me, and lets me cry.

TWELVE

For the next three nights, every time I go to sleep, I relive the crash. Over and over again, I wake up screaming and drenched in sweat, lying in the blackness of my own guest bedroom. There are no memories of the clearing left, of my mom telling me to wake up, or of Bobby showing me to my room.

By the fourth night, I get it. I may not be the brightest bulb on the porch, but I can figure out what message my subconscious is sending: **You were on the plane, stupid.**

You never walked away.

I have been like an anthropologist,

looking in darkness for evidence of a lost civilization. Maps, photographs, drawings, they all decorate the walls of my house.

But now, finally, I see the light.

I am the one who has been lost, and it's time to let go.

This is the message of my nightmares: Let go and move on or cling to fantasy and fall. My own mind has taught me the lesson that a battalion of shrinks could not. Too long has my heart been living outside my body—outside the state of California and all semblance of reality.

The next morning, I waken feeling bruised by nightmares, and I know what I must do. I totter out of bed; make a big pot of coffee and a resolution.

Inch by inch, I clear my walls. I start with the photographs of the Comfort Lodge and the map of the Olympic Peninsula. I am halfway done when my doorbell rings. I stand back, looking at my so-called progress. The entire east wall of my living room is littered with pin holes.

Tiny empty spaces where something used to be.

This is precisely the kind of thought I've been trying to avoid. When my doorbell rings again, I lunge for my crutches and head for the entry.

There, I open the door and find Stacey frowning at me.

"You look like crap."

That hurts. "Well . . . you're fat." I spin on my left crutch and step-swing into my guest room.

Although I can't hear footsteps on the carpet, I know she's following me. I go to the wall and tear down a picture of Mount Olympus.

"You're getting rid of it all?"

"Isn't that what you wanted?"

"Joy . . ."

Something in her voice gets to me. I turn around finally, face her. "I'm losing it."

Stacey sits down on my bed, and then pats a place beside her.

I hop to the bed and sit down.

"What's going on?" she asks.

"I can't sleep. Nightmares."

"Of the crash?"

I nod. "My shrink said I brought it on by going to the airport. Like I needed to hear it was my fault."

"And what about Daniel and the boy?"

I can hear the question in her voice, the wondering if she should mention the obvious. Actually, I appreciate it. There will come a time—soon, I think—when I won't want to hear their names any-more. "I haven't dreamt about them since you took me to the high school. And when I think about them, it's . . . blurry."

"What does that mean, you think? Are you getting well?"

I look down at my hands. I've thought a lot about this. A woman who can't sleep has plenty of time to contemplate. "I think . . ." I can't say it out loud.

Stacey puts her hand on mine.

Her touch steadies me. I look up. Tears burn my eyes, turn her face into a Monet painting. I'm glad. I don't want this moment to be in focus. "When I first woke up, I was sure it was all real. Daniel. Bobby. The Comfort Lodge. The rainforest. Then I heard the facts, and I knew it wasn't real, but still I **believed.** I didn't know how to stop. I wanted it all so much. I felt so alive there, so needed and wanted, and here . . ." I shrug. "I kept thinking: If only I could find my way back to them."

"And now?"

I take a deep breath, release it slowly. "I've Googled it all, and called information, and read about every town near or in the Olympic rainforest. My town doesn't exist, neither does the lodge. Therefore, it makes sense that Daniel and Bobby are imaginary, too. It was all my weird way of dealing with the pain and horror of the crash."

"That sounds like your shrink talking."

"At two hundred bucks an hour, I listen to her." I smile, but the joke falls flat.

"You're giving me logic. I want emotion."

"I can't handle emotion anymore. It's killing me. I'm too old to believe in magic and fate and destiny."

"So it was the drugs, in other words, and your own subconscious."

I frown. That's not quite right. It's important to me that I get all of this absolutely right. Otherwise I'll never be able to get past it. "I think Daniel and Bobby were . . . metaphors."

"I flunked out of tech school, remember? What do you mean?"

"I think they represent the love that could be out there for me—if I'm bold enough to change my life." I take a deep breath and say: "The truth is, Stace, I'm tired of being alone. I want love, passion, and children. All of it."

Stacey is quiet for a long time, and then says, "I can understand that."

"I know you can."

"And you deserve it," she says softly.

I glance around my walls, staring at the pattern of tack holes between the few remaining clippings. Soon, this room will be back to normal; all evidence of my impossible journey will be gone. What will I dream about then?

"Come on," Stacey says at last. "We're going to be late."

She ushers me out to the minivan. On the long drive to the doctor's office, we talk about little things, nothing that matters.

Once there, it takes less than an hour to cut off my cast, take an X-ray, and pronounce me healed. My orthopedist, Dr. John Turner, says, "The break has healed beautifully. As well as we could have hoped. And Mark says the physical therapy is going well."

"Yeah," I say.

"How much more will she need?" Stacey asks.

"I don't know." He looks at me. "We'll just take it day by day, okay? How are the headaches?"

"Better," I say. Mostly, it's true. The whiplash symptoms are abating slowly.

The appointment is winding down, edging toward goodbye, when there's a knock at the door. A woman comes into the examining room; she's carrying a white plastic bag. "Doctor?"

He looks at her. "Yes, Carol?"

"These are Ms. Candellaro's clothes. The ones they cut off her after the crash. We would have thrown them away, but there were some personal items in the pockets."

Something about that hits me hard. I don't know if it's **cut off** or **crash**. All I know is I can't smile or move.

Stacey takes the bag. "Thank you."

I'm still vaguely disconcerted as we walk through the parking lot. I'm using a cane for balance, though honestly, I think it's emotional, a phantom feeling of less than wholeness. In truth, my once-broken bone feels strong.

All the way home, I stare at the bag.

Stacey pulls into my driveway and parks. "Are you okay?"

"I will be," I say, grabbing the bag.

"I could take that for you. Get rid of it."

"I know." How can I tell her I'm not ready to get rid of it yet? Instead of speaking, I smile and nod and get out of the minivan.

Leaning heavily on the cane, I make my way up to the front door. Behind me, I hear Stacey drive away.

Inside the house, it's too quiet.

I've forgotten to leave the stereo on. I immediately go to the radio and push the button.

Bruce Springsteen is singing. "Baby, I Was Born to Run." I change stations, find a nice, soothing Elton John ballad.

No more dreams for me. I toss the bag of clothes on top of my bureau and go back to work, stripping the pictures from my wall. When I'm finished, and my butter yellow walls are a desert of tiny gray pin holes, I cram everything into grocery bags and take them out to the garbage can in my garage.

Everything goes in the trash.

A ticket to Seattle.

A white bag full of ruined clothes.

For the next week, these two items—along with the memories they represent—sit on my dresser.

I look at them every time I walk past, but I don't touch.

No way.

Until my memories of Daniel and Bobby have faded completely, I will ignore the ticket and the bag. By the time I finally reach for them, they will be cold, their power stripped by the passage of days. Someday I will pay the change fee and use my first-class ticket to fly to some other destination. Maybe Florida or Hawaii.

I am studiously ignoring the bag when the phone rings.

I answer quickly, turning my back on my dresser. "Hello?"

"Mrs. Candellaro?"

I wince at the name and all that it implies. Perhaps, my summer project will be to return to my maiden name. "Yes?"

"This is Ann Morford. How are you?"

"Fine," I say to my realtor. "You want to renew the listing?"

"Actually, I'm calling with good news. We have an offer on your house. Two hundred ninety two thousand five hundred dollars. I guess when you survived the crash, your house changed from bad luck to good luck."

"Wow." I sit on my bed, stunned.

"Do you want to make a counter offer? See if they'll come up to full price?"

It takes less than ten seconds to make

up my mind. I know a second chance when I see one. "No. I'll take the deal."

The realtor and I talk for a few more minutes about details. Earnest monies and closing dates and the like. I tell her I can be out of this house by Friday if they'd like, and I mean it. At the realization that I finally **can** leave, I'm desperate to get going. She faxes me the paperwork, which I sign immediately and re-send.

As soon as I'm done with that, I head for the kitchen to pour myself a celebratory glass of wine. I don't make it past my dresser, though.

This time, I'm caught. The sale of my house and the prospect of moving has changed things somehow. I'm finally moving, changing my direction. The idea of it makes me feel indestructible.

I grab the bag and carry it to the bed where I sit, staring down at it. Then, very slowly, I open it.

The first thing I see is my left shoe.

Just the one. I pick it up. The black-and-white Keds tennis shoe is in perfect condition. No stains or rips or mud.

My sweater has a few dark stains that I know could be either mud or blood or a mixture of both. It isn't ruined, though. A normal person, looking at this sweater would never guess its history. There's something oddly comforting in that.

Then I pull out my jeans.

The right leg has been cut and ripped from hem to waist. Dried blood makes the material stiff and discolored.

I reach into the front left pocket and pull out a wadded up Von's grocery store receipt, an airport parking stub, and seven dollars in cash. In two back pockets I find some spare change and a paper clip. Exactly the things I expected to find.

In the other front pocket, I feel something odd. I reach in farther, find something cold and hard. I pull it out and stare down at my hand.

In my palm is a small, white arrowhead.

I close my eyes and count to ten. When I look down again, the arrowhead is still there.

It can't be. You know it can't.

You didn't walk away from the crash.

Yet I'm holding this arrowhead. With everything I am, everything I think and feel, I believe this.

Of course, I've believed lots of crazy things . . .

I walk over to my bathroom and hold my hand up to the mirror.

There it is: small and white against my palm, like the tip of a Christmas tree.

I need help. Closing my hand tightly around the arrowhead, I head out of my room. As I pass the bureau, I see the airline ticket and glance at my clock. The daily flight to Seattle leaves in just under three hours.

What if?

Once again those two small words infuse my world with hope and possibility. I can't push them away, can't stop the swell of longing this time.

Shoving the ticket in my purse, I leave the house that already feels as if it belongs to someone else and go to my garage, where I limp past the file cabinets of my dreams and get into my Volvo. Behind me, the door lifts open.

Before I start the car, I look down at the thing in my hand.

It's still there.

Slowly, keeping my foot on the brake, I back out of my garage and down the driveway. All the way to my sister's house, I clutch the arrowhead and pray it's real.

I don't think my fragile mind can handle another delusion.

Still praying, I park in Stacey's driveway, grab my cane, and go to the front door, where I ring the bell repeatedly.

It isn't until I hear footsteps that I remember who else lives here and think: **This could be bad.**

Thom answers.

I stare at him, this man who held my heart for so many years and slept beside me and sometimes remembered to kiss me good night. It is the first time in months I've been this close to him, and I feel . . .

Nostalgic and nothing more. Here is my past, my youth, staring down at me. He looks remarkably like he did on the night I met him, all those years ago. Back when we were kids.

"Hey, Thom," I say, surprised at how easy it now is to say his name.

"Joy." His normally strong voice is a whisper. I can see him wondering what to say.

"It's funny how things work out," I say, giving him time to think.

"I'm sorry, Joy."

I'm surprised by how deeply his words affect me. I hadn't known until just now that I needed to hear them. "Me, too."

After that, silence falls between us.

Neither knows where our words should go. We stare at each other; he looks as sad as I feel. Finally, he says, "Is Stacey expecting you?"

"No."

He glances toward the stairs and yells, "Stace. Your sister's here."

Stacey comes down the stairs, looking panicked. She looks worriedly at Thom, then turns to me. "Are you okay?"

"I'm better than okay, actually." I grab her sleeve and pull her into the hallway. I should wait for more privacy, maybe take her to a room, but I'm too nervous and excited to be sensible. "I found this in the pants I was wearing on the plane." I lift my hand and slowly unfurl my fingers.

Stacey stares down at my palm.

I can see it as plain as day—a small white arrowhead.

Please . . . I don't even know how to finish my prayer. I just know that if my hand is empty, I'm lost. I'll need—as

they say—a long vacation in a rubber
room. It takes every scrap of courage I
possess to ask her: "Do you see it?"

"The rock?"

White hot wonder suffuses me; with
it, I can see how cold and empty I
was before. "You see it," I say. "It's really
there."

"It's an arrowhead, I think. What does
it mean?"

"It means I'm going north."

"I don't understand."

"Neither do I, but I'm using my plane
ticket."

That stops her. "Are you sure?"

"One hundred percent."

I see how her face creases at that, how
her eyes fill with fear and worry. It's the
crash. Like me, she'll battle those memories for a long time. "It won't happen
again," I say gently.

"I'm going with you."

I touch her arm. "I know it sounds
crazy, but I think I need to do it just like
I did before. Alone. Looking for hope."

"I'm driving you to the airport, then. Don't even **think** about arguing with me about it." She runs past me and goes upstairs. I can hear her moving down the hallway overhead. I return to the living room, where Thom is waiting. We stare at each other.

"Take good care of her," I say at last. "She really loves you."

"I love her, too, Joy." I hear the throatiness in his voice and know he means it.

I feel a pinch at that, a phantom pain, but it's gone quickly. "Good."

A few minutes later, Stacey reappears. Grabbing her keys from the copper bowl on the entry table, she kisses Thom good-bye, then leads the way to the garage. While she's starting the van, I get my purse and the ticket. Then I climb into the passenger seat and slam the door shut.

My sister looks at me. "Are you sure about this?"

"Absolutely."

"Okay, then. We're off."

Thirty-five minutes later, we are at the airport. We pull up to the curb and park, then get out of the minivan.

On the sidewalk, she pulls me into her arms and holds me so fiercely I can hardly breathe. "Don't you vanish on me."

"I'll call you when I get there," I promise.

"Wherever **there** is." Stacey draws back. "I'm afraid I'll never see you again."

"How can I disappear? I have a wedding to go to in June."

Stacey draws in a sharp breath. "You'll come?"

"We're sisters," I say simply.

I can see the impact of my words. Stacey smiles, but its watery and weak. "I love you, Joy."

And I know then: no matter what I find or don't find in Washington State, I will always have a place where I belong. It has taken us a long time, but Stacey and I have finally returned to the beginning. We're sisters again, two little girls in the back of a hot VW bus, experiencing our lives through each other, holding hands when we're scared.

"I love you, too, Stace."

It takes almost forty minutes to get to my gate, and then another twenty minutes before they call my flight.

I get in to line.

To my left, through the dirty bank of windows, I see my plane.

Can I do it? Suddenly, I don't know. I can feel my heart beat and the sweat popping out on my forehead.

I reach into my pocket, coil my fingers around the arrowhead.

Promise you'll come back, Joy.

It's crazy.

Head injury insane.

But I **believe.**

It's that simple, really.

Crazy or not, I believe.

Breathing carefully, moving slowly, I enter the aircraft and go to seat 2A.

There, I pull the seat belt tightly across my lap and check where the exit row is.

Then I pray.

THIRTEEN

I scream when we touch down in Seattle. The sound horrifies me, as does the obvious disapproval of my fellow passengers and the flight attendants, but I can't contain my fear until we've landed.

I am still shaking as I follow the crowd of my fellow passengers off the airplane and through the busy beige bowels of SeaTac airport. Silvery fish inlaid in the tile lead me to the baggage claim area, where I rent a sensible car and get a map of western Washington.

Outside, I finally see the famous landmarks that have become so familiar. The distant snow-capped mountains and bright blue waters of Puget Sound. Mount Rainier rises out of the mist.

I have to remind myself forcibly that I've never been here. I have done so much research on the area I could have a Ph.D.

Bumper-to-bumper traffic takes me to Tacoma, a city that is low and gray and seems to huddle beneath a layer of ominous clouds.

Olympia, the state capitol, is unexpectedly rural from the highway. Every now and then I see an official looking building, with a spire or a rotunda or columns, hidden in a thicket of trees.

By the town called Cosmopolis (wildly inappropriately named, I might add), I am in a different world altogether, where huge stacks pump noxious smoke into the sky, and peeled logs clog the waterways. Here, at the mouth of Grays Harbor, the economy is obviously based on timber and the sea, and both industries seem faded or failing. Houses are run-down, shops are closed up, the streets of the various downtowns are empty of commerce and people.

At Aberdeen, I turn inland onto old Highway 101, which promises to take me to Queets, Forks, Humptulips, Mystic, and Rain Valley.

This is it. If my dream is real, I'll find it on this road, the only one that man has built between the mighty trees of the rainforest and the gray swell of the Pacific.

I pull off the road and park, suddenly afraid.

"Get a grip, Joy," I say out loud, trying to use my best librarian's voice, but I am like one of my own students—unconvinced. With shaking hands, I open my map.

The town names taunt me. Which one of them is "my" town? Or will they all be unfamiliar? Am I looking for Daniel and Bobby and a lodge by a silver lake or was that all just a promise, a signpost to a future that hasn't begun yet? Am I supposed to find a man like

Daniel? Is Bobby the son I may some-day have?

It overwhelms me, that thought, leaves me shaken. How will I know what I'm looking for? I reach for my cell phone and call my sister, who answers on the first ring.

"Damn it, Joy, it's about time. I have no fingernails left."

"You had none to start with." I stare out the windshield at the empty road. "I don't know where to go, Stace. It all looks . . ."

"Take a deep breath."

I do.

"Again."

I draw in a deep, calming second breath and release it.

"Now," she goes on, "where are you?"

"A logging town on the coast. About an hour from the start of the National Park. What if I don't find this place I'm looking for?"

There's a crackling pause before my sister says, "You will."

"How can you believe that?"

"Because you do."

Her words sink in and settle. They give me something to cling to, remind me that though I may be crazy, I'm not alone. "Thanks."

"I'll be sitting by the phone, you understand that, right?"

"I'll call."

"Where's your first stop?"

I glance down at the map. "Amanda Park."

"That sounds promising."

It rings absolutely no bells in my head, but then again, my head is clearly unreliable. "Yeah. Talk to you later. Bye."

"Bye."

I hang up, return to the road and drive north.

As I near the start of the Olympic National Forest, the view changes. Here, the landscape is unexpectedly shorn of trees. The area along the highway has been logged and replanted, but in the distance, I can see the white-capped peak

of Mount Olympus rising into the
gray sky.

There are hardly any mailboxes along
the road, and the few homes I see are
mobile or manufactured, set back on
clear-cut lots with no hint of landscaping. Perhaps this place can't be clipped
and claimed and domesticated; it can
only be taken by force and held onto
by luck.

Amanda Park is a quaint town on the
shores of Lake Quinalt.

Neither of which I recognize. I drive
up and down the streets but nothing is
familiar, so I return to the highway and
continue north.

A sign welcomes me to Queets. I follow the old, poorly maintained road
toward the town and through it.
Nothing is familiar.

Back out on the highway, I take a
sharp turn to the right, and there is the
Pacific Ocean. Endless gray water, dap-
pled by a sprinkling of rain; white, roar-

ing waves. I pull off to the side of the road again and get out.

The driftwood is exactly as I remember it. So are the wind-sculpted trees. Only the sand is different. On my beach night, I stood in ankle-deep California pale gold sand to dance with Daniel.

In reality, the sand, like the sky and the sea today, is a shade of gray.

The entire coast is a riotous band of emerald green—huge bushes and stunted trees and mammoth ferns. I recall from my reading that it is the longest wilderness coast left in the world. Then, I was captured by the word "coast." Now, standing here, I see the word that matters is "wilderness."

As I get back into my car and drive back onto 101, I am tangled in my own emotions. Amazed by the parts of my dream that were accurate, and heartened by them, and disturbed by the pieces that were wrong.

Several more towns welcome and disappoint me. Though the landscapes are familiar, none of the towns are the one of my dreams.

As I leave the wild gray shores of the Pacific and head inland again, the landscape becomes wilder and more primitive. Here, the trees are gigantic and straight, blocking out most of the sunlight. Mist clings to the old asphalt and gives everything a mystical, otherworldly feel. I drive through town after town and find nothing that speaks to me. By late afternoon, as the golden sun sets into a cache of thick, black shadows along the roadside, my faith is beginning to fade, too.

Then I come to a sign made of sculpted metal that welcomes me to Rain Valley.

Rain Valley.

My foot eases off the accelerator. There's a nervous flutter in my stomach that I haven't felt before.

I coast forward. In a way I'm moving

against my will now, being drawn forward.

I'm afraid to believe I may have found my town . . . and more afraid that I'll be wrong again. There are only a few more turns left, here in the deep woods, and only Mystic and Rain Valley are near lakes.

I turn onto Cates Avenue and roll into Rain Valley.

In the middle of the road, I hit my brakes.

It's "my" town.

And it isn't.

I pull over to the curb and get out of the car. I can feel the moisture in the air, hear it drop from leaves and boughs and plunk into potholes in the road, but it isn't really raining. By the time I reach the sidewalk, the sun is breaking through the clouds, gilding the grassy lawn. Dew sparkles on the green carpet.

I feel as if I'm in a **Twilight Zone** episode. The town—this town—is the funhouse mirror version of my remembered town. There is a park in the center of it—but it's nothing like I imagined. There's a gazebo in the center of the park also, its stanchions twined by wisteria that is moments away from blooming. Concrete benches and fountains are everywhere. Off to the left is a covered barbeque area surrounded by picnic tables. A shallow wading pond catches the slivers of sunlight greedily; its rippling surface seems to catch fire in streaks.

Leaning on my cane, I walk across the spongy grass to the main street of town.

My town was comprised of wooden buildings with big windows and cutesy names like the Wizard of Paws pet store, the Hair Apparent beauty salon, and The Dew Drop In diner.

I stop in front of Lulu's hair salon. To my left is the Raindrop diner.

Only the ice-cream shop is exactly as I imagined it. And the church.

My version is so close that I feel weak

in the knees, and so different that I am sick to my stomach.

Was I here or wasn't I?

Am I crazy? Brain damaged?

Just as I imagined, the town is a sparkling jewel set against a backdrop of the endless Olympic forest. One million acres of trees and mountains and wilderness, without a road to drive through it. The street lamps hold hanging baskets now, their sides thick with brown vines and winter-dead geraniums. A few hardy pansies show their colorful faces.

I walk into the diner first. There is no wall of pamphlets, no man drinking coffee at the bar. There is no bar.

An older woman with a Lucille Ball–red beehive hustles toward me, smiling. "Welcome to the Raindrop. What can I do yah for?" She hands me a plastic menu.

"I . . . I'm looking for the Comfort Fishing Lodge."

The woman stops and frowns, her

heavily made-up eyes almost close completely. "Honey, I've lived here for forty years. There ain't no such place. But old Erv Egin, he'll give you a hell of a charter. Come salmon season, that is."

"Is there any fishing lodge?"

She shakes her head. "We ain't that developed yet, though the good Lord knows we could use a little tourism. There's a motel out on Fall River that makes a mighty fine breakfast, and the resort out at Kalaloch, and that place up at Lake Crescent in Port Angeles, but there ain't really fishing at any of 'em. Your best bet is a charter. In May . . ."

"Daniel?" I whisper his name, feeling like an idiot. "He has a son, Bobby."

"You talking about the O'Shea's? Out on Spirit Lake?"

My heart skips a beat. "There's a Daniel who lives on the lake? And he has a son named Bobby?"

The waitress takes a step back. She's eyeing me hard now, and I don't think she likes what she sees. Her gaze pauses on the cane, then returns to my face. "Who are you?"

"My name is Joy. I've come a long way to find them."

"They've had their share of trouble in the past few months, and then some. What with the accident and all. They don't need no more."

"I've had some trouble of my own. I wouldn't do anything to hurt them."

It seems to take forever, but the woman finally nods. "They're out at the end of Lakeshore Drive."

I can't help smiling. I even laugh a little, though it sounds hysterical. "Thanks."

I limp out of the diner. I am in my car, easing away from the curb when I realize I didn't ask for directions.

But my heart will lead me. I'm sure of it.

I drive out along the park to the old highway.

And keep going.

There's no turn off where I remember.

I drive all the way to Forks before I finally turn around. On the way back, I study every sign carefully, slow down at every one. In the old part of Rain Valley, the houses are tiny and crammed together; the streets are named after trees. None of them is Lakeshore Drive. The sun is lower in the sky now; the streets are slowly fading into shadow. There are no street lamps out here, no sign of people.

I am about to turn around again when I see a small green marker that points to Spirit Lake.

A shiver moves through me at the name. I follow the road out of town. I haven't gone more than a mile when I come to a barricade that reads: "Danger: High Water." The river has exceeded its banks and washed out a portion of the road. At least a foot of brown water runs across the asphalt.

I pull off the side of the road and park.

What now?

Is it a sign, this flooded road? Am I **not** supposed to go down to the lake?

Or am I supposed to walk? There's a strange pull in me at that answer. I walked here once, if the magic is real.

Maybe I need to repeat history to find my present. I can't help noticing that there's a huge, skinned log lying along the edge of the road. A woman with a cane could walk across that, if she wanted to.

I am crazy. Even by my own standard, and God knows my threshold has fallen to almost nothing these days.

As I sit there, hands on the steering wheel, staring at the ruined road, my cell phone rings. I know without looking at the number who it is. "Hey, Stacey," I answer.

"I've been calling for an **hour**."

"It's no-man's-land out here. I'm surprised there's service. You should see this place, it's . . ."

"I don't want a travelogue. **Well?**"

I am afraid to put it into words, this

fragile impossible hope of mine, and more afraid not to. The split between what I imagined and what I now see throws me into a kind of tailspin; I don't know what to think. "I'm parked on Lakeshore Drive. The woman at the diner said Daniel and Bobby O'Shea live at the end of the road."

"Wow," Stacey says sharply. "Is it them?"

"I hope so. Who knows? I could be Brad Pitt/**Twelve Monkeys** crazy. I'm probably still in the airport, sitting in my seat, drooling."

"You're not in the airport drooling. I watched you board the plane."

"You were there?"

"I didn't think you'd be able to do it."

"Yeah, well, I'm stronger than I used to be." As I say the words, I realize the truth of them. I **am** stronger now. Strong enough to reach for this dream . . . and strong enough to handle disappointment.

What matters is that I've finally made a move. Whether Daniel and Bobby are real or not, I belong here. Soon I will have over two hundred and ninety thousand dollars in the bank. That definitely gives me the freedom I need to start over somewhere. And this is where I want to be.

I look through the windshield. No raindrops blotch the glass. "It's time," I say to Stacey.

"Don't you vanish on me."

"I won't." Even as I say it, I can't help thinking of Bobby, to whom I made the same promise.

I hang up and toss my phone in my purse. Looping the straps over my shoulder, I get out of the car.

The world is radiant, bathed in the last, fading rays of sunlight. The trees on either side of the road are as big as I'd imagined. Many rise well over two hundred feet into the air; their trunks are as straight as flagpoles. Salal and rhododendrons grow in wild disarray amid the trunks. Moss coats everything—tree bark, branches, guardrails, rocks. Very carefully, using my cane for support, I climb up onto the log that spans the rushing water and walk to the other side. On dry land again, I limp down to the road and follow it. Walking with a cane is slow going, but not once do I pause or consider stopping.

I've gone about a mile when I hear the lake, slapping against the shore.

I turn a corner and there I am, on a cherry tree–lined driveway. At the end of the road is a sprawling old Victorian mansion with a huge covered porch. It is the kind of home that the timber barons built at the turn of the century. Even though the roof looks like a slanted mossy hillside and the porch sags dangerously to one side, it is spectacular. A hand-carved wooden sign by the entrance welcomes me to the Spirit Lake Bed and Breakfast.

There are two outbuildings on either side, small clapboard structures with broken windows and ramshackle chimneys.

No red truck with a blue door sits in the driveway.

No dock juts out over the lake.

No pile of kayaks and paddleboats lay piled by the shore.

No ruined vegetable garden shows the first signs of spring. In fact, there's no landscaping at all. There are only the cherry trees, full of pink blossoms that line the road and lead to the front door. None of it is familiar except the trees and the lake.

I have never seen this place before.

And yet, there by the lake, is the swing set, exactly as I "saw" it.

I'm crazy.

Maybe I'm not really here. The terrifying thought wings through my mind. Maybe I'm in the hospital still, on killer drugs.

In a coma.

I'm Neo in **The Matrix** before they save him.

I'm . . .

"Stop it, Joy."

It takes a monumental act of will, but I move forward.

FOURTEEN

I follow the bumpy asphalt road to its rounded end. I am just about to turn toward the house when I hear a noise. A boy's voice carried by the breeze.

Bobby.

I turn toward the sound, listening. It's him. Gripping my cane more tightly, I hurry past the swing set and go into the trees.

There he is, kneeling in his forest church, playing with action figures. Giant trees ring and protect him. Sunset slants through the great, down-slung boughs in purple-hued rays. The ferns and moss are lime green with new growth.

As I limp toward him, my heart is beating too quickly. The spongy, damp ground swallows my footsteps. So it is that he doesn't hear me approach until I say, "Hey, Bobby."

At the sound of my voice, his hands freeze. The action figures clatter together and go quiet. Slowly, he turns to look at me.

He is exactly as I've imagined him— black, curly hair, bright blue eyes with long lashes, and a missing pair of teeth.

But the way he frowns at me is new.

"Bobby?" I say after a confusing minute. "It's me. Joy."

He doesn't smile. "Sure it is."

"I'm sorry I went away, Bobby."

"Everyone said you were **imaginary** anyway."

"I guess I was then. I'm not now."

He frowns. "You mean . . ."

"I'm **here,** Bobby."

Hope flashes across his eyes. The quelling of it is the saddest thing I've ever seen. "I ain't falling for it. I don't wanna be crazy anymore."

"I know what you mean."

"Quit trying to trick me." His voice catches on that. I can see how hard he is trying to be sane and grown up. And how much he wants to believe in me again.

"I know it's impossible," I whisper. "And totally Looney Tunes, but will you trust in me one more time?"

"How?"

"Just come here."

He shakes his head. "I'm scared."

I smile. That kind of honesty will save us in this crazy situation. "Me, too. Please? Believe in me one more time." I can't help remembering my dreamed-of Christmas morning where I said the same thing to him.

Slowly, he gets up and comes toward me. When he's almost close enough to take my hand he stops. He doesn't reach for me. "Are you real?"

"That's the first thing you ever said to me, remember? Then, I didn't know what you meant, I didn't understand. But I'm real now, Bobby. Believe me."

He won't touch me, but I see that hope come back into his eyes. "You broke your promise."

"Yes, I did. And I'm sorry for that."

"How come you have a cane?"

"That's a long story."

"I waited for you to come back. Every day . . ." His voice breaks. I can see how hard he's trying not to cry.

"I have a present for you," I say softly.

"Really?"

I reach into my pocket, half expecting it to be empty.

It's not. My fingers coil around the cool, smooth bit of carved stone. I pull it out and hand it to him. The white arrowhead looks like a tiny heart in my palm.

Bobby gasps. "It's white. My mommy always promised me . . ."

I move slowly toward him and drop to

my knees in the dirt. "She showed me where it was, Bobby. On Christmas Eve night while you were sleeping."

"Really?"

I nod. "Sometimes the magic is real, I guess."

Tears glaze his eyes. I know how long he has waited for an adult to say these words to him. He takes the arrowhead from me, closing his fingers tightly around it.

"I knew it," he whispers. "I'm not crazy."

"You can keep it in your pocket always, and when you get scared or feel lost or confused, you can hold it and remember how much she loved you."

I open my arms.

He launches himself at me. I catch him easily, but lose my balance. My cane drops to the side, and we fall to the mossy ground in a tangled heap. For the first time, I'm really holding him.

His kiss on my cheek is slobbery and wet . . . and real.

"Hey," he says, drawing back, "you're warm."

"I wasn't before?"

He shakes his head solemnly. "When you touched me, it was like . . . the wind."

We sit up, look at each other. "Hey, Bobby O'Shea. It's nice to really meet you."

"I thought you were like . . . Mommy. Gone."

I touch his cheek; it is softer than I ever imagined. "No. It just took me a long time to find my way back."

"How were you here?"

I wonder if there will ever be an answer to that. If I will someday know why my dream was a flawed and tattered version of reality or how I ended up here when I was hooked up to machines in a white bed in Bakersfield. For now, all I can do is shrug and say the thing I do know. "Magic."

He thinks about that. "Okay."

The resilience of children. If only we

could hold onto that. I smile. "So, what have you been doing since I left?"

He grabs my hand and gets to his feet. "Come on." Tugging hard, he leads me out of the clearing and toward the house. I can tell he's impatient with my speed, but the cane and my limp will only allow me to move so fast. I laugh and beg him to slow down.

As we move through the yard, I notice how shadowy everything is here on the edge of the deep woods; night falls quickly here, unlike in my dream world where everything seemed to go slowly.

Bobby tightens his grip on my hand and veers left. We go around the house and up a small rise. There, behind the house are five small cabins. Two are obviously old, and three are of brand new construction.

He goes to the closest one—a new one—and opens the door. I follow him inside, stumbling over the threshold.

It's dark in here. Behind me, he flicks a switch and light comes on.

We are in a small, beautifully con-
structed cabin with wide plank pine
flooring, unfinished walls, and big mul-
lioned windows that overlook the lake.
To the left, a door is partway open; in the
space, I can see a bathroom tiled in white
with a claw-foot tub.

"He didn't know what to do with the
walls. It wasn't on the list."

"Oh." I'm confused. Before I can
question him, he re-takes my hand and
leads me out of the cabin.

"He fixed 'em all up and built the new
ones. 'Cause of you."

"I don't know what you're talking
about, Bobby, I . . ."

He stops and looks up at me. "You
know. The list."

"What list?"

He reaches into his shirt pocket, pulls
out a worn, yellow piece of paper. It ap-
pears well worn, as if refolded endlessly.
He opens it, hands it to me. "We look at
it every day."

I look down at the well-used piece of paper.

> *Ibeas.*
> chng nme/rmantic
> pant trm
> flwrs
>   fix cbns
>   websit
>   no crpt flr

"Oh," I whisper, shivering although I'm not cold. "How . . ."

Bobby shrugs. We both know there is no answer to my unvoiced question. It's like the arrowhead: magic. As impossible as it is, some part of me was here, and I left these words behind.

"I told my daddy you'd come back," he says quietly. When he looks up at me, I am filled with a kind of love I've never known before.

I bend down and take him in my arms, holding him tightly.

He is the first to pull away. It couldn't have been me.

"Come on," he says, taking my hand again, pulling me toward the house. As we cross the yard, a wind kicks up. Suddenly the world is full of falling petals. It's snowing pink.

At the door, Bobby stops and grins up at me. "Let's surprise him."

"Oh, it'll be a surprise," I say, feeling my stomach knot up. It is one thing to get a boy to believe in magic; it's another thing entirely to pin such impossible hopes on a full-grown man.

Bobby knocks on the door. Footsteps rattle inside the house.

I tighten my hold on his hand.

The door opens and Daniel is there, looking almost exactly as I pictured him. He is not quite as lean as I imagined, and his hair is shorter.

But it's Daniel, all right.

Bobby is moving from foot to foot so excitedly, he seems to be dancing the

Macarena. I, on the other hand, am as still as stone. "Look, Daddy. She's back."

I try to smile, but can't. All he has to do is shut the door or turn away and I'll be lost. "Open the damn door," I say, my voice catching on the swear word, just as Bobby had known it would. "It's cold out here."

"Joy?" I hear the confusion in Daniel's voice, the disbelief.

Bobby laughs. "I **knew** he'd know you."

I don't understand. "How do you recognize me?"

"Bobby drew about a million pictures of you," he says in that lovely brogue of my dreams. "And he talked about you 'til I couldn't stand it anymore. But . . ."

"But what?"

"You're beautiful."

Heat climbs up my cheeks. I feel like a teenager, being noticed by the football captain for the very first time. It is a feeling I thought I'd never experience again. "This is insane," I whisper.

"Joy." The way he says my name is like a prayer. It wrenches my heart and gives me hope.

Without thinking, I move toward him, put my hand on his arm. My cane falls to the floor in a clatter, forgotten.

He touches my face, and only then, when I feel the heat of his palm against my cold cheek do I realize how keenly I wanted him to reach for me. His touch is the gentlest I've ever known. I sigh, seeing a pale cloud of my breath.

"I feel as if I already know you."

I nod. It's crazy, but I feel it, too.

"So, who are you, really?"

"Joy Faith Candellaro. I'm a high school librarian from Bakersfield."

"Joy Faith, huh? That's a grand name." He steps back, makes a sweeping gesture with his hand. "Well, come on in."

I step past him and limp into the house. I can feel him staring at me, and I know he has a dozen unanswerable questions—I know because I've asked them of myself—but just now I'm caught between worlds, the here and there of my dream and this reality.

There is no registration desk. That's the first thing I notice. No wall of old-fashioned keys, no counter full of bro-chures and tourist maps. Like Rain Valley, some of what I saw was real and some was pure imagination. I don't know how to make sense of it.

I turn to my left and see the lobby. **The living room.**

Just as in my dream, there is a huge stone fireplace.

The decorations Bobby and I put on the mantel are still there—the polyester pile of glittery snow, the cast resin homes and stores, the mirror skating pond and horse-drawn carriages. In the corner of the room, exactly where I put it, is a Christmas tree, draped in lights and or-naments. Beneath it, a lone package sits.

The single present is long and thin. It's crudely wrapped and held together by big strips of masking tape. JOY is written on it in red crayon. It is a present for me.

And that's when it hits me: I never had Christmas this year. My holiday was spent in a white room that smelled of disinfectant and flowers. There had been no magical holiday morning, no presents to open, and no unending games of Monopoly.

No one saved Christmas for me.

Until now. Tears sting my eyes but don't fall. Of all the people in my life, these two—strangers in the real world— have saved the holiday for me. How is that possible? Or isn't it?

"It's March," I say, looking up at Daniel. Suddenly I'm afraid again that it's all a lie. "I'm in a coma somewhere, aren't I?" I step back from him.

"He never stopped believing," Daniel says to me. "He wouldn't have Christmas without you."

"But the tree . . ."

"It's our sixth one."

I limp past him to the tree. I need to feel its pointy needles, smell its sharp fragrance.

These are the decorations he put up, one by one, the mementos of his young life. **That one was Mommy's favorite . . . I made it in day care.**

There's a new ornament on the branch nearest me. It's a small picture frame, formed of fired, painted clay. The kind of thing a child would make at one of those pottery places. Inside the red-and-green frame is a stick figure painting of three people—a dark haired man with a big smile, a curly-haired boy, and a red-haired woman. Below the people are our names, written in an adult's careful hand: Daniel, Bobby, and Joy.

"I made it for you," Bobby says, grinning. "But Daddy helped."

I turn to Daniel. My heart feels swollen suddenly, tender. I don't know what to say to this man who is both a friend and a stranger.

I feel myself starting to cry. It makes

me look like a fool, to be moved by something so small, and by people whom I barely know, but I can't stop the swell of emotions. I've felt alone for so, so long now, and now—however impossibly— I feel as if I've finally come home. "You must think I'm crazy . . ."

Daniel wipes the tears from my cheek. "You know what's **really** crazy?" he says in a voice so low that only I can hear.

"What?"

"A man my age believing in magic." He puts his hand around the back of my neck and pulls me in close. "I don't know how this whole thing happened, or where we go from here, but I know one thing: We've been given a gift." Leaning down to kiss me, he says, "Merry Christmas, Joy Faith Candellaro. We've been waiting for you."

It is a quick kiss, a touching of lips and nothing more, but it reaches deep inside me, warms a place that has been cold for a long time. I lean into him, put my arms around his neck. As if from a distance, I hear a little boy giggle.

"Come on, Joy," Bobby says. "You have a present to open."

And I smile. Here and now. It is the best present of my life.

I look up at Daniel and whisper, "Magic," and I know that for the rest of our lives we will believe.

Read on for an exciting preview of

KRISTIN HANNAH'S

Magic Hour

Available in hardcover
Spring 2006 from

THE RANDOM HOUSE
PUBLISHING GROUP

It will all be over soon.

Julia Cates had lost count of the times she'd told herself that very thing, but today—finally—it would be true. In a few hours the world would know the truth about her.

If she made it downtown, that was. Unfortunately, the Pacific Coast Highway looked more like a parking lot than a freeway. The hills behind Malibu were on fire again, and smoke hung above the rooftops and turned the normally bright coastal air into a thick brown sludge. All over town terrified babies woke in the middle of the night, crying gray-black tears and gasping for breath. Even the surf seemed to have slowed down, as if exhausted by the unseasonable heat.

She maneuvered through the cranky, stop-and-go traffic, ignoring the drivers who flipped her off and cut in front of

her. It was expected; in this most dangerous of seasons in Southern California,
tempers caught fire as easily as backyards.
The heat made everyone edgy.

Finally, she exited the freeway and
drove to the courthouse.

Television vans were everywhere.
Dozens of reporters huddled on the
courthouse steps, microphones and cameras at the ready, waiting for the story to
arrive. In Los Angeles it was becoming a
daily event, it seemed; legal proceed-
ings as entertainment. Michael Jackson.
Courtney Love. Robert Blake.

Julia turned a corner and drove to a
side entrance, where her lawyers were
waiting for her.

She parked on the street and got out
of the car, expecting to move forward
confidently, but for a terrible second she
couldn't move. **You're innocent**, she reminded herself. **They'll see that. The
system will work.** She forced herself to
take a step, then another. It felt as if she
were moving through invisible wires,

fighting her way uphill. When she made it to the group, it took everything she had to smile, but one thing she knew: it looked real. Every psychiatrist knew how to make a smile look genuine.

"Hello, Dr. Cates," said Frank Williams, the lead counsel on her defense team. "How are you?"

"Let's go," she said, wondering if she was the only one who heard the wobble in her voice. She hated that evidence of her fear. Today, of all days, she needed to be strong, to show the world that she was the doctor they'd thought she was, that she'd done nothing wrong.

The team coiled protectively around her. She appreciated their support. Although she was doing her best to appear professional and confident, it was a fragile veneer. One wrong word could strip it all away.

They pushed through the doors and walked into the courthouse.

Flashbulbs erupted in spasms of blue-white light. Cameras clicked; tape rolled.

Reporters surged forward, all yelling at once.

"Dr. Cates! How do you feel about what happened?"

"Why didn't you save those children?"

"Did you know about the gun?"

Frank put an arm around Julia and pulled her against his side. She pressed her face against his lapel and let herself be pulled along.

In the courtroom, she took her place at the defendant's table. One by one the team rallied around her. Behind her, in the first row of gallery seating, several junior associates and paralegals took their places.

She tried to ignore the racket behind her; the doors creaking open and slamming shut, footsteps hurrying across the marble tiled floor, whispered voices. Empty seats were filling up quickly; she knew it without turning around. This courtroom was the Place To Be in Los Angeles today, and since the judge had disallowed cameras in the courtroom, journalists and artists were no doubt packed side by side in the gallery, their pens ready.

In the past year, they'd written an endless string of stories about her. Photographers had snapped thousands of pictures of her—taking out the trash, standing on her deck, coming and going from her office. The least flattering shots always made the front page.

Reporters had practically set up camp outside her condo, and although she had never spoken to them, it didn't matter. The stories kept coming. They reported on her small-town roots, her stellar education, her pricey beachfront condo, her devastating breakup with Philip. They even speculated that she'd recently become either anorexic or addicted to liposuction. What they didn't report on was the only part of her that mattered: her love of her job. She had been a lonely, awkward child, and she remembered every nuance of that pain. Her own youth had made her an exceptional psychiatrist. It was, really, the only thing that mattered to her.

Of course, that bit of truth had never made it to press. Neither had a list of all the children and adolescents she'd helped.

A hush fell over the courtroom as Judge Carol Myerson took her seat at the bench. She was a stern-looking woman with artificially bright auburn hair and old-fashioned eyeglasses.

The bailiff called out the case.

Julia wished suddenly that she had asked someone to join her here today, some friend or relative who would stand by her, maybe hold her hand when it was over, but she'd always put work ahead of socializing. It hadn't given her much time to devote to friends. Her own therapist had often pointed out this lack in her life; truthfully, until now, she'd never agreed with him.

Beside her, Frank stood. He was an imposing man, tall and almost elegantly thin, with hair that was going from black to gray in perfect order, sideburns first. She'd chosen him because of his brilliant mind, but his demeanor was likely to matter more. Too often in rooms like this it came down to form over substance.

"Your Honor," he began in a voice as soft and persuasive as any she'd ever heard, "the naming of Dr. Julia Cates as a defendant in this lawsuit is absurd. Although the precise limits and boundaries of confidentiality in psychiatric situations are often disputed, certain precedents exist, namely **Tarasoff v. the Board of Regents of California**. Dr. Cates had no knowledge of her patient's violent tendencies and no information regarding specific threats to named individuals. Indeed, no such specific knowledge is even alleged in the complaint. Thus, we respectfully request that she be dismissed from this lawsuit. Thank you." He sat down.

At the plaintiff's table, a man in a jet-black suit stood up. "Four children are **dead,** Your Honor. They will never grow up, never leave for college, never have children of their own. Dr. Cates was Amber Zuniga's psychiatrist. For three years Dr. Cates spent two hours a week with Amber, listening to her problems and prescribing medications for her growing depression. Yet with all that intimacy, we are now to **believe** that Dr. Cates didn't **know** that Amber was becoming increasingly violent and depressed. That she had no warning whatsoever that her patient would buy an automatic weapon and walk into her church youth group meeting and start shooting." The lawyer walked out from behind the table and stood in the middle of the courtroom.

Slowly, he turned to face Julia. It was the money shot; the one that would be drawn by every artist in the courtroom and shown around the world, "**She** is the expert, Your Honor. She should have foreseen this tragedy and prevented it by warning the victims or committing Ms. Zuniga for residential treatment. If she didn't in fact know of Ms. Zuniga's violent tendencies, she should have. Thus, we respectfully seek to keep Dr. Cates as a named defendant in this case. It is a matter of justice. The slain children's families deserve redress from the person most likely to have foreseen and prevented the murder of their children." He went back to the table and took his seat.

"It isn't true," Julia whispered, knowing her voice couldn't be heard. Still, she had to say it out loud. Amber had never even **hinted** at violence. Every teenager battling depression said they hated the kids in their school. That was light-years away from buying a gun and opening fire.

Why couldn't they all see that?

Judge Myerson read over the paperwork in front of her. Then she took off her reading glasses and set them down on the hard wooden surface of her bench.

The courtroom fell into silence. Julia knew that the journalists were ready to write instantly. Outside, there were more of them standing by, ready to run with two stories. Both headlines were already written. All they needed was a sign from their colleagues inside.

The children's parents, huddled in the back rows in a mournful group, were waiting to be assured that this tragedy could have been averted, that **someone** in a position of authority could have kept their children alive. They had sued everyone for wrongful death—the police, the paramedics, the drug manufacturers, the medical doctors, and the Zuniga family. The modern world no longer believed in senseless tragedy. Bad things couldn't just happen to people; someone had to pay. The victims' families hoped that this lawsuit would be the answer, but Julia knew it would only give them something else to think about for a while, perhaps distribute some of their pain. It wouldn't alleviate it, though. The grief would outlive them all.

The judge looked at the parents first. "There is no doubt that what happened on February nineteenth at the Baptist church in Silverwood was a terrible tragedy. As a parent myself, I cannot fathom the world in which you have lived for the past months. However, the question before this court is whether Dr. Cates should remain a defendant in this case." She folded her hands on the desk. "I am persuaded that as a matter of law, Dr. Cates had no duty to warn or otherwise protect the victims in this set of circumstances. I reach this conclusion for several reasons. First, the facts do not assert and the plaintiffs do not allege that Dr. Cates had any specific knowledge of identifiable potential victims; second, the law does not impose a duty to warn except to clearly identifiable victims; and finally, as a matter of public policy, we must maintain the confidentiality of the psychiatrist-patient relationship unless there is a specific, identifiable threat which warrants the undermining of that confidentiality. Dr. Cates, by her testimony and her records and pursuant to the plaintiffs' own assertions, did not have a duty to warn or otherwise protect the victims in this case. Thus, I am dismissing her from the complaint, without prejudice."

The gallery went crazy. Before she knew it, Julia was on her feet and enfolded in congratulatory hugs by her defense team. Behind her, she could hear the journalists running for the doors and down the marble hallway. "She's out!" someone yelled.

Julia felt a wave of relief. **Thank God.**

Then she heard the children's parents crying behind her.

"How can this be happening?" one of them said loudly. "She should have known."

Frank touched her arm. "You should be smiling. We won."

She shot a quick glance at the parents, then looked away. Her thoughts trailed off into the dark woods of regret. Were they right? **Should** she have known?

"It wasn't your fault, and it's time you

told people that. This is your opportunity to speak up, to—"

A crowd of reporters swarmed them.

"Dr. Cates! What do you have to say to the parents who hold you responsible—"

"Will other parents trust you with their children—"

"Can you comment on the report that the Los Angeles District Attorney's Office has taken your name off the roster of forensic psychiatrists?"

Frank stepped into the fray, reaching back for Julia's hand. "My client was just released from the lawsuit—"

"On a technicality," someone yelled.

While they were focused on Frank, Julia slipped to the back of the crowd and ran for the door. She knew Frank wanted her to make a statement, but she didn't care. She didn't feel triumphant. All she wanted was to be away from all this . . . to get back to real life.

The Zunigas were standing in front of the door, blocking her path. They were paler versions of the couple she'd once known. Grief had stripped them of color and aged them.

Mrs. Zuniga looked up at her through tears. "You did help her, Dr. Cates."

"She loved both of you," Julia said softly, knowing it wasn't enough. "And you were good parents. Don't let anyone convince you otherwise. Amber was ill. I wish—"

"Don't," Mr. Zuniga said. "Wishing hurts most of all." He put an arm around his wife and drew her close to him.

Silence fell between them. Julia tried to think of more to say, but all that was left was **I'm sorry,** which she'd said too many times to count, and "Good-bye." Holding her purse close, she eased around them, then left the courthouse.

Outside, the world was brown and bleak. A thick layer of smoke darkened the sky, obliterating the sun, matching her mood.

She got into her car and drove away. As she merged into traffic, she wondered if Frank had even noticed her absence. To him it was a game, albeit with the biggest stakes, and as the day's winner, he would be flying high. He would think about the victims and their families, probably tonight in his den, after a few Dewar's over ice. He would think about her, too, perhaps wonder what would become of a psychiatrist who'd so profoundly compromised her reputation with failure, but he wouldn't think about them all for long. He didn't dare.

She was going to have to put it behind her now, too. Tonight she'd lay in her lonely bed, listening to the surf, thinking how much it sounded like the beat of her heart, and she'd try again to get beyond her grief and guilt. She **had** to figure out what clue she'd missed, what sign she'd overlooked. It would hurt— remembering—but in the end she'd be a better therapist for all this pain. And then, at seven o'clock in the morning, she'd get dressed and go back to work.

Helping people.
That was how she'd get through this.

Girl crouches at the edge of the cave, watching water fall from the sky. She wants to reach for one of the empty cans around her, maybe lick the insides again, but she has done this too many times already. The food is gone. It has been gone for more moons than she knows how to keep track of. Behind her the wolves are restless, hungry.

The sky grumbles and roars. The trees shake with fear, and still the water drips down.

She falls asleep.

She wakes suddenly and looks around, sniffing the air. There is a strange scent in the darkness. It should frighten her, send her back into the deep, black hole, but she can't quite move. Her stomach is so tight and empty it hurts.

The falling water isn't so angry now; it is more of a spitting. She wishes she could see the sun. Life is so much better when she is in the light. Her cave is so dark.

A twig snaps.

Then another.

She goes very still, willing her body to disappear against the cave wall. She becomes like the shadow of herself, flat and motionless. She knows how important stillness can be.

Him is coming. Already he has been gone too long. The food is no more. The sunny days are past, and though she is glad Him is gone, without Him, she is afraid. In a time—long ago now— Her would have helped some, but she is **DEAD**.

When the forest falls silent again, she leans forward, poking her face into the gray light Out There. The darkness of sleepnight is coming; soon it will be blackness all around. The falling water is gentle and sweet. She likes the taste of it.

What should she do?

She glances down at the pup beside her. He is on alert, too, sniffing the air.

She touches his soft fur and feels the tremble in his body. He is wondering the same thing: Would Him be back?

Always before Him was gone a moon or two at the most. But everything had been changed when Her got dead and gone. When Him left, he actually spoke to Girl.

YOUBEGOODWHILEI'MGONE ORELSE.

She doesn't understand all of the words, but she knows Or Else.

Still, it is too long since he left. There is nothing to eat. She has freed herself and gone into the woods for berries and nuts, but it is the darkening season. Soon she will be too weak to find food, and there will be none anyway when the white starts falling and turns her breath into fog. Though she is afraid, terrified of the strangers who live Out There, she is starving, and if Him comes back and sees that she has freed herself, it will be bad. She must make a move.

*   *   *

The town of Rain Valley, tucked between the wilds of the Olympic National Forest and the roaring gray surf of the Pacific Ocean, was the last bastion of civilization before the start of the deep woods.

There were places not far from town that had never been touched by the golden rays of the sun, where shadows lay on the black, loamy soil all year, their shapes so thick and substantial that the few hardy hikers who made their way into the forest often thought they'd stumbled into a den of hibernating bear. Even today, in this modern age of scientific wonders, these woods remained as they had for centuries, unexplored, untouched by man.

Less than one hundred years ago, settlers came to this beautiful spot between the rain forest and the sea and hacked down just enough trees to plant their crops. In time they learned what the Native Americans had learned before them: this was a place that wouldn't be tamed. So they gave up their farming tools and took up fishing. Salmon and timber became the local industries, and for a few decades the town prospered. But in the nineties, environmentalists discovered Rain Valley. They set out to save the birds and the fish and the eldest of the trees. The men who made their living off the land were forgotten in this fight, and over the years the town fell into a quiet kind of disrepair. One by one the grandiose visions of the town's prominent citizens faded away. Those much-anticipated streetlights were never added; the road out to Mystic Lake remained a two-lane minefield of thinning asphalt and growing potholes; the telephone and electrical lines stayed where they were—in the air—hanging lazily from one old pole to the next, an invitation to every tree limb in every windstorm to knock out the town's power.

In other parts of the world, in places where man had staked his claim long ago, such a falling apart of a town might have dealt a death blow to the citizens' sense of community, but not here. The people of Rain Valley were hardy souls, able and willing to live in a place where it rained more than two hundred days a year and the sun was treated like a wealthy uncle who only rarely came to call. They withstood gray days and springy lawns and dwindling ways to make a living, and remained through it all the sons and daughters of the pioneers who'd first dared to live among the towering trees.

Today, however, they were finding their spirit tested. It was October seventeenth, and autumn had recently lost its race to the coming winter. Oh, the trees were still dressed in their party colors and the lawns were green again after the brown days of late summer, but no mistake could be made: winter was coming. The sky had been low and gray all week, layered in ominously dark clouds. For seven days it had rained almost nonstop.

On the corner of Wheaton Way and Cates Avenue stood the police station, a squat gray-stone building with a cupola on top and a flagpole on the grassy lawn out front. Inside the austere building, the old fluorescent lighting was barely strong enough to keep the gray at bay. It was four o'clock in the afternoon, but the bad weather made it feel later.

The people who worked inside tried not to notice. If they'd been asked—and they hadn't—they would have admitted that four to five consecutive days of rain was acceptable. Longer if it was only a drizzle. But there was something **wrong** in this stretch of bad weather. It wasn't January, after all. For the first few days, they sat at their respective desks and complained good naturedly about the walk from their cars to the front door. Now, those conversations had been pummeled by the constant hammering of rain on the roof.

Ellen Barton—Ellie to her friends, which was everyone in town—stood at the window, staring out at the street. The rain made everything appear insubstantial, a charcoal rendering of town. She caught a glimpse of herself in the water-streaked window; not a reflection, precisely, more of a feeling played out momentarily on glass. She saw herself as she always did, as the younger woman she'd once been—long, thick black hair and cornflower blue eyes and a bright, ready smile. The girl voted homecoming queen and head cheerleader. As always when she thought about her youth, she saw herself in white. The color of brides, of hope for the future, of families waiting to be born.

"I gotta have a smoke, Ellie. You know I do. I've been really good, but it's reaching critical mass about now. If I don't light up, I'm heading to the refrigerator."

"Don't let her do it," Cal said from his place at the dispatch desk. He sat hunched over the phone, a sheath of black hair falling across his eyes. In high school Ellie and her friends had called him the Crow because of his black hair and sharp, pointed features. He'd always had a bony, ill-put-together look, as if he wasn't quite at home in his body. At almost forty, he still had a boyish appearance. Only his eyes—dark and intense—showed the miles he'd walked in his lifetime. "Try tough love. Nothing else has worked."

"Bite me," Peanut snapped.

Ellie sighed. They'd had this same discussion only fifteen minutes ago, and ten minutes before that. She put her hands on her waist, resting her fingertips on the heavy gun belt that was slung across her hips. She turned to look at her best friend. "Now, Peanut, you know what I'm gonna say. This is a public building. I'm the chief of police. How can I let you break the law?"

"Exactly," Cal said. He opened his mouth to say more, but a call came in and he answered it. "Rain Valley Police."

"Oh, right," Peanut said. "And suddenly you're Miss Law and Order. What about Sven Morgenstern—he parks in front of his store every day. Right in front of the hydrant. When was the last time you hauled his car away? And Large Marge shoplifts two boxes of freezer pops and a bottle of nail polish from the drugstore every Sunday after church. I haven't processed her arrest papers in a while. I guess as long as her husband pays the tab it doesn't matter. . . ." She let the sentence trail off. They both knew she could cite a dozen more examples. This was Rain Valley, after all, not downtown Seattle. Ellie had been the chief of police for four years and a patrol officer for eight years before that. Although she stayed ready for anything, she'd never processed a crime more dangerous than breaking and entering.

"Are you going to let me have a cigarette or am I going to get a doughnut and a Red Bull?"

"They'll both kill you."

"Yeah, but they won't kill **us,**" Cal said, disconnecting his call. "Hold firm, El. She's the patrol clerk. She shouldn't smoke in a city building."

"You're smoking too much," Ellie finally said.

"Yeah, but I'm eating less."

"Why don't you go back to the salmon jerky diet? Or the grapefruit one? Those were both healthier."

"Stop talking and answer me. I need a smoke."

"You started smoking four days ago, Peanut," Cal said. "You hardly **need** a cigarette."

Ellie shook her head. If she didn't step in, these two would bicker all day. "You should go back to your meetings," she said with a sigh. "That Weight Watchers was working."

"Six months of cabbage soup to lose ten pounds? I don't think so. Come on, Ellie, you know I'm about ready to reach for a doughnut."

Ellie knew she'd lost the battle. She

and Peanut—Penelope Nutter—had worked side by side in this office for more than a decade and been best friends since high school. Over the years their friendship had weathered every storm, from the ruination of Ellie's two fragile marriages to Peanut's recent decision that smoking cigarettes was the key to weight loss. She called it the Hollywood diet and pointed out all of the stick-figure celebrities who smoked.

Grinning at Cal, she placed her hands on the desk and pushed herself to a stand. The fifty pounds she'd gained in the past few years made her move a little slower. She walked over to the door and opened it, although they all knew there'd be no breeze to suck the smoke away on such a wet and dismal day.

Ellie went down the hall to the office in the back that was technically hers. She rarely used it. In a town like this, there wasn't much call for official business, and she preferred to spend her days in the main room with Cal and Peanut. She dug past the signs from last month's pancake breakfast and found a gas mask. Putting it on, she headed back down the hall.

Cal burst out laughing.

Peanut tried not to smile. "Very funny."

"I may want children someday. I'm protecting my uterus."

"If I were you, I'd worry less about secondhand smoke and more about finding a date."

"She's tried everyone from Mystic to Aberdeen," Cal said. "Last month she even went out with that UPS guy. The good-looking one who keeps forgetting where he parked his truck."

Peanut exhaled smoke and coughed. "I think you need to lower your standards."

"You sure look like you're enjoying that smoke," Cal said with a grin.

Peanut flipped him off. "We were talking about Ellie's love life."

"That's all you two ever talk about," Cal pointed out.

It was true.

Ellie couldn't help herself: She loved men. Usually—okay, always—the wrong men.

Peanut called it the curse of the small-town beauty queen. If only Ellie had been like her sister and learned to rely on her brains instead of her beauty. But some things simply weren't meant to be. Ellie liked having fun; she liked romance. The problem was, it hadn't yet led to true love. Peanut said it was because Ellie didn't know how to compromise, but that wasn't accurate. Ellie's marriages—both of them—had failed because she'd married good-looking men with itchy feet and wandering eyes. Her first husband, former high school football captain Al Torees, should have been enough to turn her off men for years. But she'd had a short memory and just a few years after the divorce she married another good-looking loser. Poor choices, to be true, but the divorces hadn't dimmed her hopes. She still believed in romance and was waiting to be swept away. She knew it was possible; she'd seen that true love with her parents. She lifted the gas mask and said, "Any lower, Pea, and I'd be dating out of my species. Maybe Cal here can set me up with one of his geek friends from the comic book convention."

Cal looked stung by that. "We're not geeks."

"Yeah," Peanut said, exhaling smoke. "You're grown men who think other men in tights look good."

"You make us sound gay."

"Hardly." Peanut laughed. "Gay men have sex. Your friends wear **Matrix** costumes in public. How you found Lisa, I'll never know."

At the mention of Cal's wife, an awkward silence stumbled into the room. The whole town knew she was a runaround. There was always talk; men smiled, women frowned and shook their heads at the mention of her name. But here in the police station, they never spoke about it.

Cal went back to reading his comic book and doodling in his sketch pad. They all knew he'd be quiet for a while now.

Ellie sat down at her desk and put her feet up.

Peanut leaned back against the wall and stared at her through a cloud of smoke. "I saw Julia on the news yesterday."

Cal looked up. "No kidding? I gotta turn on the TV more."

Ellie reached behind her head and pulled off the mask. When she set it on the desk, she couldn't help sighing. It had only been a matter of time before they came around to the subject of her brilliant younger sister. "She was dismissed from the lawsuit."

"Did you call her?"

"Of course. Her answering machine

had a lovely tone. I think she's avoiding me."

Peanut took a step forward. The old oak floorboards, first hammered into place at the turn of the century when Bill Whipman had been the town's police chief, shuddered at the movement, but like everything in Rain Valley, they were sturdier than they appeared. The West End was a place where things—and people—were built to last. "You should try again."

"You know how jealous Julia is of me. She especially wouldn't want to talk to me now."

"You think everyone is jealous of you."

"I do not."

Peanut gave her one of those **Who-do-you-think-you're-fooling?** looks that were the cornerstone of friendship. "Come on, Ellie. Your baby sister looked like she was hurting. Are you going to pretend you can't talk to her because twenty years ago you were homecoming queen and she belonged to the math club?"

In truth, Ellie had seen it, too—the haunted, hunted look in Julia's eyes—and she'd wanted to reach out and help her younger sister. Julia had always felt things too keenly; it was what made her a great psychiatrist. "She wouldn't listen to me, Peanut. You know that. She considers me only slightly smarter than a pet rock. Maybe—"

The sound of footsteps stopped her.

Someone was **running** toward their office.

Ellie got to her feet just as the door swung open, hitting the wall with a **crack**.

Lori Forman skidded into the room. She was soaking wet and obviously cold; her whole body was shaking. Her kids—Bailey, Felicia, and Jeremy—were clustered around her. "You gotta come," Lori said to Ellie.

"Take a breath, Lori. Tell me what's happened."

"You won't believe me. Heck, I've seen it and I don't believe me. Come on. There's something on Magnolia Street."

"Yee-**ha,**" Peanut said. "Something's actually happening in town." She reached for her coat on the coatrack beside her desk. "Hurry up, Cal. Forward the emergency calls to your cell phone. We don't want to miss all the excitement."

Ellie was the first one out the door.

About the Author

KRISTIN HANNAH is the best-selling author of many acclaimed novels, including **On Mystic Lake, Between Sisters,** and **The Things We Do for Love.** She lives in the Pacific Northwest with her husband and son.